The Witch of Sawtooth Mountain

The Witch of Sawtooth Mountain

Dorothy Nickerson

Scythe Publications, Inc.

A Division of Winston-Derek Publishers Group, Inc.

PUBLISHED BY SCYTHE PUBLICATIONS, INC.
A Division of Winston-Derek Publishers Group, Inc.
Nashville, Tennessee 37205

Library of Congress Catalog Card No: 94-060453
ISBN: 1-55523-690-1

Printed in the United States of America

This story is dedicated to all the readers who love our Lord, and know that good always triumphs over evil in the end.

⌐ Chapter One ⌐

Ann sank down gratefully on an old hickory log and gazed out through the blue haze of Pine Ridge. Easing back against the trunk of a red gum tree, she savored its pungent aroma. A raccoon watched her from behind the branches of a sassafras bush, his beady, black eyes never wavering. The Ozarks were beautiful in the fall, but their beauty hardly eased the hardships of living in the crude cabin she and her husband John shared.

Suddenly she doubled up her fist and beat on the log, frightening the raccoon into flight. Why did she leave her comfortable life in Denver? This is a backward place, and it is full of stupid people who don't give a damn about us. She must be insane. Aunt Cora had tried to talk her out of it, but love won out. Her eyes burned with tears as she pounded the log again.

Small and dark, of French parents, Ann had a million dollar shape. Why hadn't she taken the modeling job, or sung with the dance band in Denver? She had been raised by her mother's sister after her parents were killed in their plane. Aunt Cora had told her sister she was flirting with death riding in that crazy machine. Ann remembered begging to go along... sometimes now she wished she had.

She remembered the parties, the beautiful gowns she wore, and the admiring glances from all the boys. Aunt Cora tried to make a lady of her by taking her to all of the social events, and exposing her to all of the right people. Later on, when she met Bill at a charity ball, all of her training was forgotten.

Her aunt almost had a heart attack when she learned Ann was staying with him on weekends. After a few weeks, however, the arrangement had become permanent. Even now when she thought of Bill, his dark charm seemed to invade and envelop her. How could she have left the life she had shared with Bill? He had treated her like a doll and had always tried to please her. Why hadn't she married him instead?

Aunt Cora thought it was a blessing when Ann met a handsome seminary student, John, at one of the charity affairs.

"Ann, I would like you to meet one of our fine young men from the seminary," her aunt's friend had said. Then she found herself drowning in smiling blue eyes, and her hands imprisoned in his strong, vibrant hands.

"My name is John Nilson," his mouth was saying, but his eyes were holding hers and saying much more. Miracles seemed to happen as they sat on the patio drinking in each other's words. "Ann," he told her finally, "I have been looking for someone like you all of my life."

"But, John, you don't know me," she protested in alarm.

"I know you," he smiled. And in that moment she somehow knew he was her future.

After that day, she started planning how she could break off with Bill. She knew it would be hard. He would not want to give up anything he considered his property. Little by little she began taking her personal treasures out of his apartment. Most of her clothes however were still there. She still remembered the ugly scene the day she finally told him.

"I'll get you back," he threatened. "No man can love you like I do!" His dark face flushed with anger. "Don't worry, I'll find you too!" he vowed as he smashed an expensive vase against the door. Trembling, she ran out without her things and hailed a cab.

Because of John's appointment to Gentry here in the Ozarks, their marriage had been hurried. He had been more than honest with her.

"Ann, this is a remote area without electricity, or inside plumbing. Do you think you can put up with that kind of life?" She had assured him that the main thing was being with him. She felt she had been living in a dream from the day she had met him. Warmth filled her heart as she thought of his strong arms around her, and his kind voice chasing away all of her doubts. His love was like a soft blanket, and she knew nothing could hurt her as long as he loved and believed in her.

It had taken a month of this bleak place to erase the glow, and the waking up had been painful. Tears of self-pity now washed her face. What a raw deal to be stuck here in this primitive place. It was not what she had dreamed of for her life. Suddenly, determination routed her dark mood and her blood began to boil. Shaking her fist at the trees she announced, "I'll make it here if it kills me."

Her thoughts of home and Aunt Cora reminded Ann that she might get a letter today. She would have to check their box out on the trail. She had written her aunt to send her some hand and face cream. The store in Gentry did not handle such luxuries, and these hill women would not know how to use them anyway. She couldn't even find a decent bar of soap. As she started along the path her long hair caught on a bramble. She did not notice the old hill woman and almost fell over her while trying to get loose.

"Oh, I am sorry," Ann began. "I didn't expect to meet anyone up here."

"Heh, heh, I jest bet ye didn't," the old woman replied. "Now I aim to give ye fair warning", she said as she bent down and picked up a stick. "There ain't a bit of use fer ye and the preacher to stay, so ye had best git! We'uns don't need you here."

Ann shrank back from the old woman's malice. The hill woman's back was bent, but her piercing eyes were bright as she waved the stick wildly. Ann felt a hot flush of anger grip her as she fell back on a log.

"There ain't no use for ye to get het up," the old woman continued as she spit tobacco juice on the ground. "Ye ain't the first do-gooders thet has tried to take over my hollers. I done sent them packing, and ye might as well git ready to go too!" she added. Then, raising her stick, she began to beat Ann. Quickly, Ann decided to run for it. At the first turn she paused and looked back. She could not see the old woman anywhere, and guessed she had gone the other way.

Ann walked on to the mailbox all the while wondering about the old crone. Looking in their mailbox was a relief when she found a letter from home. Hurrying back to the cabin, she sank into the big rocker. Aunt Cora's letter made her want to cry. The little church close to Denver that John had spoken of before being called to Gentry was now needing a pastor. She would ask him to take it and maybe they could get back to civilization.

When John rode in that evening she still felt a little shaken, but he looked so tired that she decided not to mention her aunt's letter. She did tell him about the old woman and was surprised by the alarm on his face.

"Ann, you are not to leave this cabin unless I am with you," he warned. "I'll inquire around and see if anyone knows who she is." Taking her in his arms he held her close. "Honey, these past weeks have been the happiest I have ever known. I could not stay here and do this work if I didn't have you."

Flushing with remorse she hugged him back and decided to wait with her news. Taking the water bucket out to the back porch, she felt afraid of the darkness. She was glad the cistern was handy, and not out in the yard. She did not intend on being caught by surprise by the old hill woman again. Next time she intended to fight back.

On Sunday she and John were invited to dinner with the Wilks family after services. Since John was married, most of the families usually did not bother to invite him to eat. However, Hattie Wilks had a daughter, Lettie May, to whom Ann had been kind, and Ann thought they must be trying to return the favor.

As John helped Ann into the Wilks' wagon, she shuddered to think of riding very far over the rocky trails in the rickety thing. To her surprise the ride was not bad at all. The bed of the wagon was cushioned by deep piles of sweet-smelling meadow grass. Hattie's man, Jess, was balding and had a profusion of red beard. He sang a lively song with Lettie May almost all of the way. As they approached a bend Ann could see a cabin and heard the baying of a hound.

"That be old Tick welcoming us home," Jess explained.

"How does he know it is you?" Ann asked.

"Why any good hound knows the sound of his own wagon," Jess laughed. "If he don't, he'd jest be still and wait."

As they came closer, Ann could see the cabin clearly. It had never known paint and the chimney sagged as if weary from long service. Near the gate a lone rose bush struggled to live. In the back were the remains of a garden and a few scraggly apple trees. She thought it was the poorest place she had ever seen for people to be living.

"We got as pretty a place as there be around these hills," Jess stated with pride. "This here was my Pappy's a'fore me, and it will be Lettie May's someday when she gits herself a man."

"Now Pa, ye hush up. Our Lettie could have her pick just any time she's a'mind to. Shore wish you could have seen my garden," she announced proudly. "I had the best stand of peas fer miles around. We got over two hundred jars in the cellar, counting everything. Course, Lettie May was a big help to me, what with poor Jess hurting his back and all. I've had to do all the hoeing and picking too."

"I shore got me a good womern," Jess stated as he spit tobacco juice at the hind end of the mule.

John gave the mountain woman a warm smile. "It helps to have a good wife," he answered as he winked at Ann.

Ann wondered if he would feel that way if he knew all about her. She saw Hattie catch her look and hoped she could not read her mind. She worried about how long she could play this goody-goody role.

As they entered the cabin she was surprised at how clean everything looked. The bare, pine floor had been scrubbed until it looked almost white. The old wood stove had been blackened, and the plank table was covered with flowered oilcloth. Glancing into the front room she saw a pieced quilt, the pride of every woman in the Ozarks.

"Jest ye set down while I dish up the vittles, Mrs. Nilson," Hattie said as she tied an apron around her ample waist. "Jess, take the preacher out back and show him the new calf. Lettie May, ye best run to the cistern fer a bucket of fresh water. Ye never tasted such good water as ours," she declared to Ann. Watching as she set out the heavy crockery, Ann remembered the fragile china from her aunt's home. Then Hattie broke in on her thoughts.

"Them vittles ought to be jest right," she said. "I left the fire banked to keep everything nice and warm. Hope you like apple pie, cause we got lots of apples. Jess puts them down in the cellar in barrels and they keep most all winter long."

"That is John's favorite pie," Ann reassured her.

"That shore is lucky fer me," Hattie smiled, her blue eyes twinkling. Opening the back screen she hollered, "You fellers come wash up so we can eat while it be hot." Her ample bosom heaved from the exertion.

John and Ann took their places on the long bench against the wall and John asked the blessing.

"Now ye jest dig right in," Hattie invited, and passed a huge platter of chicken.

"What kind of greens are these?" John asked, sampling a dish new to him.

"That be poke salad," Jess explained. "We been eating it fer as long as I recollect. It jest grows wild. I reckon the good Lord knew us poor folks would get hungry," he added, laughing and slapping his leg at his joke.

When she was helping Hattie clean the table, Ann asked her about the old woman she had met in the woods.

"That sounds like Granny Shook. Ye hain't met up with her a'ready?" Hattie asked in surprise. "She be jest plain trouble. Don't ever cross her. Folks say she has powers, and some even run after her when they got sick ones."

"I hope I never see her again," Ann replied. "She sure scared me. Now John says I can't go out walking alone anymore, and I love to walk down by the creek."

"Jest listen to the preacher, and don't go alone at all," Hattie cautioned. When they joined the men on the front porch, Jess was playing his fiddle and Lettie May was clapping time her hands. Ann thought of concerts she had attended in Denver and the velvet dresses she had worn. Glancing down at her plain cotton dress, she frowned. Would she ever dress like that again?

"Jess, you play so well. Where did you learn?" John asked the mountain man, noticing his rough hands.

"Wal, guess I jest come by it natural like. Daddy and Grandpa used this here fiddle, and I been hearing it most all my life." John marvelled at the way he could finger the instrument so fast. Swaying back and forth, his beard seemed to keep time too. It was then that the old hound lifted her nose to the breeze.

"Somebody's coming," Jess stated. Tick bayed and soon they saw a wagon and mule coming around the bend in the trail. A man and boy were riding on the spring seat. As soon as they pulled up to the gate Jess was there to meet them.

"Shore hope it hain't Jennie's time," Hattie said with a frown. "Guess it can be at that. Did you ever help git a young'un?" she asked, turning to Ann.

"Why, no," Ann answered weakly, "but I took First Aid in college. Isn't there a doctor in Gentry?"

"We never bother with a doctor much up here," the mountain woman laughed. "It takes half a day to come from Siloam Springs, even if he would. Now what's the matter, Will, is Jennie down?" she called.

"She thinks ye best come, Hattie," the big man answered. "Shore want to git back a'fore dark. Hain't no moon tonight and the trail be bad." Will was a heavy man with dark hair and a stringy beard.

The boy was fair and very thin. Ann did not recall seeing them before at church services.

Hattie turned back to the cabin and called, "Lettie May, round up the rest of that cornpone, and get me a mess of them sweet taters. Jennie never has half enough to eat fer them poor little young'uns of hers." She glanced at the man in the wagon with contempt. Ann wondered what the matter was as she looked at him and the boy. "Mrs. Nilson, why don't ye come along and help? It could take most the night though, but ye might jest get Will to bring his passel of young'uns to preaching. Lord knows it won't do him no harm neither."

Ann looked at John in alarm. He surely wouldn't expect her to be a midwife too! Still the logic of Hattie's request registered, and while she was trying to think of a good excuse she heard John agree. What kind of a mess was she getting into? Catching John's eye, she put a smile on her face.

"Fine, thet's jest fine," Hattie beamed. "I'll get some clean rags, fer like as not Jennie hain't got ary a one. Best get ye a sleeve as it be real chilly come sundown."

Ann gave up and decided she was caught up in fate. She felt a new low as the wagon bounced over the rocky trail. Nothing in her life had prepared her for such an ordeal as this.

"Hattie, have you done this many times before?" she asked.

"Law, yes!" the mountain woman exclaimed. "Guess I helped get half the young'uns around here. I shore do hope that shiftless Will got in some firewood. Like as not there ain't a stick cut and poor little Luke cain't hardly heist the ax a'tall," she added, keeping her voice low, and watching Will up on the spring seat.

Ann looked up at the frail boy swaying and holding on for dear life. Poor kid, so thin and pale. After bumping over the trail for what seemed like an hour, they came to a ramshackle cabin with a lean-to on the back. Even in the dusk she could see it was the worst looking place she had seen yet. A lamp was lit and she saw several small faces at the window.

"Now Luke, go see if you can round up some kindling," Hattie directed. "Mrs. Nilson, you help me with these things." Hattie hurried in and Ann followed hesitantly. Inside she saw a frail woman propped up in the front room bed, surrounded by three little girls. She also saw how dirty the floor was. What a terrible place to live and raise children, she thought.

"Well now, Jennie," Hattie smiled at the pale woman in the bed, "Are you about ready fer a party? I brought somebody with me. This here's the new preacher's wife, Mrs. Nilson. Guess you and Will hain't got to meet them yet. She wanted to come and help." Ann heard the concern in Hattie's voice as she asked, "How do you feel now, Jennie?"

The hill woman opened her eyes listlessly and her answer seemed almost too much of an effort. "Don't feel like much, Hattie. Jest don't see how I can manage this time. Will hain't even dug them taters yet, and Luke cain't get up in them apple trees hardly a'tall. Can ye think on sparing Lettie May fer a spell when I can make it up? Maybe she can hep me can some of them old hens a'fore the coons gits them all." Pausing for breath, she went on. "Will never did get around to fixing thet old henhouse. Sometimes I think there be no use in trying no more. Hain't much use as I can see. But I do thank ye kindly for coming." She smiled wanly in Ann's direction, then turned her face to the wall. Ann saw her dabbing at her eyes with the quilt.

"Now don't ye fret, Jennie," Hattie answered. "Everything will look a heap better come morning and it is all over." Then she sat down on the bed and smoothed the damp hair back from Jennie's face.

Ann's heart contracted with sympathy. How could God allow such want and misery to go on? How terrible it must be to be married to this shiftless man, Will. John was so wonderful… she felt she did not appreciate him enough. God, she thought, don't let him ever regret marrying such a dumb, city girl. Looking at the little girls, she called them over and asked their names.

"That there one is Mittie, this here one is Lucy, and this'n is Mary," Jennie told her. "Shore hope the next is a boy so he can be a help to Will." She closed her eyes wearily. "Don't know why I need any more young'uns no how."

"You must not feel that way," Ann remonstrated. "God will take care of you. My husband, John, says He sees every little bird that falls." She stopped. She could not believe what she had just said. John's religion must be rubbing off on her!

"Well, He ain't never bothered much over me yet," Jennie complained to Ann.

"Have you ever asked Him to help you, Jennie?" Ann asked. Then she remembered her own situation, and thought what a hypocrite she was.

"I guess I jest been too tired lately to think much on God," the little woman answered. "We used to get old Granny to hep with birthings and such, but last time we jest called on Hattie. That old woman like to have scared little Luke out of his wits the night little Mary was borned."

Ann wished she would have continued on more about Granny Shook, but decided not to ask. She helped Hattie put the food they brought on the old plank table. Every time she thought about her encounter on the trail with Granny Shook, she grew angry. Next time she met up with that old hag she intended to get in the first lick. Seeing the little girls eating cold cornbread and fried potatoes made her feel bad. Ann couldn't stand to live like this. The cabin she shared with John seemed like heaven compared to this, and they always had plenty to eat.

After the children were in bed, she heard Will snoring in the lean-to behind the kitchen. Hattie smiled and told her she might as well try and get some sleep too.

"Won't you need me?" Ann objected.

"Not for awhile, I'm a'feared," Hattie answered. "Looks to me like it is going to be hard for Jennie this time. Ye best stretch out here on a pallet by the stove. Be sure and chunk up that fire. I'll stay by Jennie."

Trying to sleep was impossible and Ann's thoughts ran wild. How could sweet, loving John have done such a mean trick? She didn't belong here in this filthy cabin. She almost wished she was back in Bill's clean apartment. Then John's hurt face flashed across her mind and she knew she could never enjoy that luxury again. Her thoughts were interrupted by sounds coming from Jennie's room. Going to the door, she was met by Hattie.

"Fetch that kettle here and chunk up that fire, Mrs. Nilson," she ordered. "Poor Jennie's not doing so good. I'm right worried. Maybe we best hunt up Will's bottle."

"I thought you said, or I said, God would help her?" Ann countered. "Oh Hattie, I am sorry. Where does Will hide it?"

"Why, Mrs. Nilson, I jest never thought on asking God to help," the hill woman said slowly, "and I jest don't rightly know why because I know how." She knelt beside the plank bench, with Ann standing self-consciously beside her. Then her gaze was drawn to the window. There framed in the darkness behind the dirty pane was the evil face of the old woman she had met on the trail. As she tugged on Hattie's sleeve, the vision faded. Rushing to the door she pulled it open and stood on the step.

"What do you want?" she called in fright and anger. The cold wind whipped her legs as if in derision. Granny Shook was gone.

"Ye must have jest been dreaming," the hill woman chided. "That old woman was way up by the mill the last I heard. Now let's us git busy and git this young'un born."

To Ann, the night seemed forever and it wasn't until the sun had risen over Pine Ridge that she heard the faint cry of the new baby. Helping Jennie drink strong black coffee, Ann told her, "It's a fine boy. He looks so sweet."

Jennie smiled at her weakly. "Mrs. Nilson, I jest know I'd never made it if you and Hattie hadn't come," she said. "Jest as soon as I can ride that wagon, we'uns shore will come to meeting. Ye can count on it. I'll see to it that Will brings us!" She looked down at the baby with love. "I reckon the preacher won't care fer me borrowing his name. We hain't never had no John in our family fer as far back as I can recollect. My, it has a good solid ring to it!"

"I think that will make John very happy," Ann told her. It would too, she knew.

It was late afternoon before Ann arrived back at the parsonage. Hattie thanked her for going along and Will seemed grateful as he helped her down from the wagon. She looked around her cabin with new eyes: the vines on the porch were really very pretty; the braided rugs gave it a rustic charm; and even the heavy water bucket seemed cool and clean. Maybe she could learn to like this place, as long as John loved her. Slowly she took Aunt Cora's letter from its hiding place and shoved it in the ashes of the stove. With a sigh she watched the coals ignite it. Then the sound of John riding in on the mare brought her back to the present.

"Well, dear," he began as he came in with an armload of wood, "how did you get along with the Perkins family last night? Do you think you will make a good nurse?" He dumped his load of wood in the woodbox.

Ann thought about the stark reality of the night before and of Jennie's needs. She also thought of the many others living in the hills and hollows. So many others needed John's help.

"Oh yes, John," she heard herself saying. "I am going to really try and be a good pastor's wife."

The relief on John's face and the love in his blue eyes was worth more to her then than all of the electric irons, lights, or pretty dresses in the world. She felt a closeness to him then that was new, and an ambition that was strange.

"John, the baby was named for you and he is so sweet," she told him. "They do need so much. We must go and check on them soon. Maybe I could help clean up that dirty place." She shuddered inwardly, thinking of her hands. She had always been so proud of her long, beautiful hands. They weren't so nice now, and she wished she had some lotion.

"We sure will," John agreed. "I need to learn how to split

wood. Nights will soon be cold and I can't ask Jess to keep us in wood all winter."

Ann went to bed that night feeling content one minute and uneasy the next. Her dreams were disturbed by vague warnings and once she awoke in real pain. She remembered the old woman and the hate she had seen in her piercing eyes. Not wishing to disturb John, she lay there quietly and tried to sleep again. Finally the shadows began to fade and she had reason to get up and get the stove going.

⊰ Chapter Two ⊱

Two or three weeks after the birth of the Perkins' baby, Ann noticed a tall, thin boy in a coonskin cap walking down the trail with a sack on his shoulder. His dark hair hung to his shoulders and she saw with surprise that he was barefoot. Watching through the window, she wondered who he was. Many of the men went barefoot all summer, but it was now September and the mornings were cold with a heavy dew. For her money he was a looker. He must be on the way to Gentry, the small settlement five miles away. The general store there was a wonder to every child around. She had been initiated a few weeks back when they had run out of sugar. There she had seen everything from mule harnesses to pretty flannel and lace. There was even an ice house where huge blocks of ice cut from the lake in the winter were stored all summer.

This morning John left early, saying he wanted to check on a family with a sick child. He would come back by way of the Perkins' cabin. She was glad. Someone ought to see to them-just as long as it wasn't her. She wondered about the boy, Luke.

Ann had not seen him since the day his little brother was born. The memory of that night made her shudder. In spite of her good intentions, she had not been back. If she had her own horse, she could visit more. But what a letdown! Her society friends would laugh if they ever found out. Not one of them would understand. And Bill... she vowed not to think about him. But she could not help but think of the big bathtub, all the hot water, and the radio in his apartment. Feeling sorry for herself, she decided to sit out on the porch. This is such beautiful country, she thought, yet so little beauty exists in these people's lives. Even in this remote place there was gossip and it found its way into every cabin, causing misery and heartbreak. Only yesterday John told her of a young girl, who was in a family way, whose father was going to turn her out.

"Do they know who the father is?" Ann asked. "What a dreadful thing to do to your own daughter."

"They say it could have been one of the survey crew that worked here early this spring," John explained. "It doesn't matter who he is, it's the girl who needs help now. Her name is Kate, and she is Eli Tate's daughter. I was thinking maybe you and I should ride over and talk to the family. She can't hire out and won't have any place to go."

Ann thought about John's words and wondered what they could do. There were homes in Denver for unwed mothers, but they wouldn't take in a girl from so far away. She smiled grimly, thinking that women were no different here than anyplace else. They were so stupid when it came to loving a man. Hearing the raucous cries of bluejays on the trail, she saw John riding in on the sorrel mare. He was so handsome in his rough blue jeans and flannel shirts. She knew the people here resented city clothes, so she had packed away all of her pretty things.

"Hi there," she called. "You are home early. Hope you aren't hungry because I have been sitting out here daydreaming."

"I've had coffee and pie already. You know it is impossible to refuse an offer of pie," he laughed. "I guess it's my weakness. Could we ride over to the Childers'? I heard they have taken Kate Tate in for awhile. Something needs to be done for her and I feel we should go and see about her."

Oh sure, Ann thought, any stray cat, dog, or human in trouble should let the preacher know, and he would take them in. Going into the cabin she took herself to task. She should not even think such things. This was his job, and she had to do her part and help, but why did it make her so mad?

As they rode over the ridge, Ann breathed in the aroma of autumn. Trees that had been verdant recently were now a riot of color. It was almost as if they were riding in a fairyland, where golden light from the sun sifted down on them through yellow, red, and orange leaves. High on the crest of a ridge, an eagle watched them from his perch on a dead pine. Ann felt the stillness, as if all the world was waiting for something to happen. She felt winter in the air and knew it would be here soon.

The Childers' cabin was like others in the hills. The front room was kept for company and the large kitchen was dominated by the iron cook stove. However, this cabin boasted a wide lean-to across the back in addition to the usual front railed porch. It was larger than most of the places she had visited. Effie was waiting out on the porch as they drove up in the wagon. Ann did not see Effie's husband, Bud. He must be off with his hound.

"Jest tie your horse to that post, Preacher," she directed. "Then you and Mrs. Nilson come on in and get warmed up." Effie was so happy to see them that she reminded Ann of a puppy. She was glad to go into the warm kitchen. She looked around for Kate but saw no one. Effie was setting out cups of steaming coffee when John came in. She was not a pretty woman but she had a wealth of soft, brown hair, and her wide smile softened her weathered face. Wearing a bun on top of her head and enveloped in an apron, she fell into the sameness of most of the married women. Her blue eyes twinkled at John.

"My, hit shore is good to see ye and Mrs. Nilson. Bud and me was jest saying this morning thet he ought to go by and see how ye be fixed for cordwood before the snow flies," Effie said as she placed a pitcher of thick cream on the table. "Bud is down to the bottomland now, digging them sweet taters."

"That would be nice of Bud and we could use some wood," John replied. "Is Kate down there too? We really came over to find out how we can help."

"She shore is and so is Dan. He played off this morning. Said he felt bad. He'd a'heap rather fool around with Bud and that old hound than ever set foot in the schoolhouse."

"Can't say I blame him for that," John smiled. "We have felt bad about Kate ever since I first heard about her last week from Yancey. We think you folks are being very kind to help her out and let her stay here in your home."

"War nothing to hit, jest mostly doing what had to be done," Effie replied. "Some don't hold with us taking her in, but Bud and me know Kate is a good girl. That city feller jest ought to be horse-whipped, if'n a body jest knew whar he be."

Ann was acutely aware of the fine qualities of the little hill woman. Effie had not been touched by civilization, and was the better for it. She had a loving spirit and a kind soul.

John savored his coffee. Nobody in the world made coffee as good as the women did here. After awhile he put his cup down.

"I hear that Kate's father is quite bitter," he began.

"Thet mean old man don't deserve a sweet girl like Kate," Effie snapped. "How his poor wife, Lucy, ever stands it living with thet mean, honery, old varmint, I cain't fer the life of me see! Guess she jest be caught and she ain't got nowhere else to go." Slanting a look at John she added, "Don't ye reckon the church house would cave if that old Eli ever set foot in it? I shore bet it would!"

"Now, Mrs. Wilks, you know God never gives up on anyone and we shouldn't either," John said. "I'm ashamed I have not visited them before now and I intend to ride up and see them soon. How far is it and which trail do I take?"

"Wal, if ye be bound to go," Effie started, "ye ride out past Hattie's and on to the ridge about two mile. If ye do go, try and git Eli to let ye have Kate's trunk. She told me she has some hope-chest things in it. Law knows she be needing quilts and things no matter where she be and them things are hers."

"We'll do that Effie and we'll try to go right away. What I really want to know is what Kate's plans are now, and how long you folks will keep her."

Effie looked down at the worn oilcloth on the table. "I purely cain't say, Preacher. Seeing as how my Mary is here, she is going to be wondering about Kate… you see with no man of her own. Hit would be a sight better if we'uns could find her someplace else whar there be no young'uns to git interested and all."

John's face was drawn with concern. Surely he is not thinking of taking Kate to the parsonage, Ann thought in alarm. But in her heart she already knew what the outcome would be. Well, she had been an assistant midwife, maybe she could do it again.

As they rode home John was very quiet and Ann knew he was trying to find the words to ask her about Kate. Finally she decided to help him out.

"I know what you are worrying about, John, and it's fine with me," she said. She was amazed at how easy the words came out. "I'm sure she can be of help to us. But what will she do after her baby comes? No one around here will ever let her forget."

"Now, dear," he replied with obvious relief, "let's not worry yet about that." His face looked so happy, she felt ashamed of her thoughts. He was so good, not at all like Bill. She remembered the cross examinations she had endured because of Bill's jealousy. She also remembered his parting threat that he would find her wherever she went.

John built a fire that evening while she put away the jams and jellies that Effie had given her. There was blackberry, tart plum, and purple grape. Effie and Mary had spent days walking the bottom land picking the fruit. Ann thought of all the cordwood Bud had split to trade for the sugar. She had been amazed at the rows and rows of jams, jellies, pickles, vegetables, and meat stored in the hill womens' cellars. For taste, city stores could not compete.

Early the next day John decided they should visit Kate's parents. The mare tossed her head in frustration in having to pull the wagon again so soon. There was a chance they might get Katie's trunk, so they needed the wagon, and Ann could go too.

She gazed at the hazy outline of Sawtooth Mountain against the early morning sky. Smoke from the cabins in the hollow curled lazily above the tops of the pines that were still wet with morning mist. Even the squirrels seemed to pause in their work of gathering nuts to watch them go by. This sure beats the sights in Denver, Ann thought. The scenery was great here, but it was the people that made her so impatient.

As they drove around a bend in the trail, they saw the cabin of Eli and Lucy Tate. It looked well-kept and the sheds in back were in good repair. As John pulled the mare up to the gate, the cabin door opened a crack. Ann saw a little woman nervously wiping her hands on her apron.

"Good morning," John called. "Are we at the Tate home? I am Pastor Nilson and this is my wife, Ann."

The hill woman opened the door a few more inches. "This here be Eli's cabin but he ain't to home jest now. He be down on the creek hunting that hog of ourn. She busted out agin last night and Eli thinks she be down there rooting our sweet taters."

"Then you must be Lucy, Kate's mother," John asked.

"I shore am, but Eli don't hold with her no more and we don't call her name around here no more. Ye can come in if ye want, or ye can drive down whar he be." She seemed to hope they would go on.

"We would like to talk to you about Kate," John told her, helping Ann down from the wagon. "We understand you have her trunk here and that she will need the things in it. Surely you don't feel that way toward your daughter."

"Hit won't do me a whit of good to feel sorry fer her. When Eli makes up his mind, the good Lord cain't change him. He don't hold none with a bad girl and poor Kate done ruint herself with her Pa."

Ann realized that the defeated little woman would be of little help to Kate now. She doubted the poor woman had ever stood up for her own opinion. How awful to have to live with such a bully. He would not get away with such meanness if he was her husband. Just then the baying of a hound floated up to them on the breeze.

"You best come on in and set," the little woman said nervously, edging back inside. "I hear Eli now, and best he don't find ye standing out on the porch." She opened the door enough so that they could enter.

John and Ann stepped into the neat, warm kitchen and sat on a bench by the stove. John told her, "We have been thinking about asking Kate to stay with us for awhile. Ann could use the company and the help during the coming winter. We thought we could get her trunk today and take it to the Childers' place."

"I'd be mighty pleased if'n she could stay at yore place," Lucy answered, finally smiling at Ann. "Hit would shore be a relief fer me. I purely hate to see Katie leave, Preacher, but I cain't do a thing in this world to help her."

Ann's eyes filled with tears of anger. Eli must be a terrible person. Then the back door opened and Eli came in. To Ann's surprise, he was a small man, barely taller than Lucy. Without a glance, he took off his coat and cap, hung them on a peg behind the stove, and proceeded to wash his hands. Then he turned toward Lucy.

"And who might these strangers be that ye have let into my cabin?" he scowled.

"I am the new pastor here, Mr. Tate," John spoke up. "My name is John Nilson and this is my wife, Ann." Lucy was nervously wiping her hands again on her long apron. Ann felt a surge of sympathy for her. She wondered if Eli had ever hit her, for she saw real fear in Lucy's face.

"I don't hold much with preachers," Eli responded. "We believe the Good Book, and too bad there ain't more thet do. Lucy and me read hit every day sitting here at our table. Don't need to go traipsing clear across the holler to hear some city feller read hit." Eli made up for his size with his loud voice and piercing dark eyes. His bushy eyebrows, long hair, and beard made Ann think of a lion. Against her will she was in awe of him.

"We would like to see you come with your wife sometime anyway, Mr. Tate," John persisted. "However, we are here today in behalf of Kate. We would like to take her trunk back to her. We hope to have her stay with us this winter when I have to be away. I hate to leave Ann alone, especially at night."

The little man turned on John furiously. "Don't reckon this be any business of yours! She made her bed, now let her lay in it! Kate don't need no molly-coddling. The Lord means fer her to pay fer her sinning, and He shore will make her suffer too."

Ann could not hold it in another minute and exploded. "You certainly can't mean this, Mr. Tate," she objected. "Kate is your daughter, and I think you are the one who is sinning when you kick her out like this."

"Not the way she has," he shouted, turning his gaze on Ann.

"Ye listen ter me, fer no good will come of ye meddling in this. Ye can have her trunk and I hope I never see hit agin, nor Kate nuther!" He then walked back to the lean-to and pulled out an old brass-bound trunk. Lucy cowered in her rocker by the stove moaning, "Don't say hit, Eli."

If he heard his wife he showed no sign, but dragged the old trunk into the kitchen. Finally he turned and hollered at her. "I hain't going to have no woodscolt brung home fer me to raise."

Ann went over and put her arm around the bent little woman. "Don't you worry Lucy, we'll take good care of Kate. I believe in time Mr. Tate will get over his disappointment and will love Kate again."

"Thank ye, Mrs. Nilson, but ye jest don't know Pa. Hit's shore a load off'n me though to know she be going to stay with y'all. When the baby comes I'm coming to see hit, if'n I have to walk." As she said the brave words, she was watching and hoping Eli had not heard. She wiped her eyes on her apron, and tried to gather up the hair that had fallen down from her bun. Eli glared at them and gave a parting threat as he went out the back door.

"Ye best watch out fer old Granny. She don't like city folks coming up here. If ye take in Kate, she'll shore be on your trail."

He didn't need to tell them that, Ann thought. She would love to leave tomorrow if she could. Then looking at her strong and moral husband, she knew it was not possible.

"Pa's right," Lucy whispered as they went out to the porch. "She be the one to say Pa should turn Kate out."

"What right does she have to do that?" John asked.

"She thinks she be God A'mighty," the little woman looked around nervously. "Jest be careful and watch out." She darted back inside and put the bar on the door.

As they drove on back, John decided to go ahead and take Kate's trunk home with them. By now, the Childers must have told Kate about their offer and he felt sure she would accept.

Late that afternoon Ann looked out and saw the young man she had noticed the day before. He was wearing boots, a bright blue shirt, and his hair had been cut. Calling to John, Ann asked if he knew who he was.

"Must be Tom Matthews," John guessed. "He lives on this side of Burnt Creek with his mother. It seems his father has been dead a long time. They don't do much farming, but I hear that he traps and is the best fisherman around. The hill men say he is always reading instead of any hunting. I'd like to know him and go fishing with him sometime."

"Oh quick," Ann begged, "call him over. He looks different from all the others here."

Urged on by the eagerness in Ann's voice, John hurried out to the road. Ann watched him talking with the young man, then they both turned back on the path leading to the parsonage. As they came in the kitchen door, she tried to look surprised.

"Tom, I'd like you to meet my wife, Ann," John said. "She thinks I need a fishing trip and I hear you know the good spots."

Tom Matthews flushed with pleasure. Standing tall and straight, his clear grey eyes smiled down at her, and she knew he was not an ignorant hillbilly.

"Yes, mam, I'd be honored to take the Preacher fishing most any day he would like. Right now is the best time, before it's too cold and wet to sleep out. The rainy season starts soon, then it is miserable. There is nothing like fishing to settle a man's doubts about himself."

"Don't tell me that you have any doubts about anything?" John asked.

"Sure do, Preacher. Can't seem to unravel the why of me or anything else. Ma says I been reading too many books and maybe she is right. Anyway, whenever you are ready, just give me the word, or ride on up to our place any morning. It's about three miles up the creek. We are the only cabin on the way up to the mill."

"Thanks, Tom," John accepted, liking the young man's looks more and more. "I have been wishing I could catch a fish ever since Ann and I first came. Would you believe I have never been fishing in my life?"

"That hardly seems possible, Preacher," Tom replied . "I am going to enjoy showing you some nice places."

"Maybe we could go next Sunday after service," John asked eagerly. "If you and your mother could come to services, you could have dinner with us."

"Ma don't get out much, Preacher. You see, she can't ride our old mule, and we don't own a wagon. I generally pack our supplies in on the mule. This time I walked as I didn't need to pack much. I love to walk and I spent the night visiting with Yancey. You come on up any day and I'll be looking for you."

John and Ann watched him start up the trail with a steady gait, the sack of supplies riding easy on his broad shoulder. Before the trail turned out of view, he turned and waved as if he knew they were watching.

"Well, what do you think of him?" John asked, smiling. "Does he measure up to your romantic notions of the handsome mountain man?"

"He sure beats the local lazy bums I've met so far." Ann watched his face for some sign of jealousy, but could see it never entered his mind.

"His speech is different. That probably comes from reading so much. Maybe I'll learn more about him and his mother when I go to their place next week."

Ann was thinking about more lonesome days. It would be so nice to hear good music and dance again. And a beer wouldn't be bad either. What a hypocrite she was. How could she be so sweet and good one minute and hating her life the next?

Getting out a box of keepsakes, she began rummaging through them. There was a picture of Aunt Cora holding her hand when she was young, a faded rose she had worn at graduation, pearls that had belonged to her mother, and an opal bracelet Bill had given her at Christmas. The opals flashed against the yellow gold. Slipping it on, she was shocked by the roughness of her arm and she took it off just as John walked in the room. Had he seen it? Guiltily, she shut the box.

"I was just looking through some old things from home. I guess you are hungry. I should get something ready for dinner," she said as she hurried to the kitchen. She did not see the hurt look on his face.

Her mind was still on Denver as she began setting out the food. It would be so nice not to have to worry about either Granny Shook, or poor pregnant girls, or what these people thought of her. As she slammed some wood into the stove she knew she had done this to herself. How could she be sweet and good one minute, and hate her life the next? She hoped fervently it would not show as she called John to supper.

⊰ Chapter Three ⊱

The next Sunday at church Ann got her first look at Kate. The Childers' family filed in with Dan and Bob first, then Mary, who looked about twelve. She was followed by another girl who did not look much older. Surely this was not the notorious Kate. She was little more than a very thin child. Her dark face was so frightened that Ann felt like hugging her. She saw the furtive glances of the people, and their frowns of disapproval. This poor girl was a disgrace as far as these local, righteous women were concerned. When the service was over, Effie brought Kate over to Ann.

"Mrs. Nilson, this here is Kate. We been telling her about ye. Do ye know this be the first time she be in the meeting house since old Grandpa Tate was buried? Must be five years back. Katie, Mrs. Nilson and the Preacher want to talk with ye." The girl kept her eyes fixed on the floor, and seemed unable to look at Ann.

"So this is Kate," Ann said, smiling as she came to the girl's rescue. "John and I have been looking forward to meeting you.

You see, we need someone to help us. When we heard about you, we asked Bud if you might want to come over and talk about it."

Kate brightened immediately. "If hit be housework I'd be right proud, but that be all I'd be fit fer. I can sew and cook right well, and Ma learned me crochet."

"Kate, that just sounds great. You can be company for me when John has to be away." Ann realized this could keep her mind off the past. "John," she called as the last straggler left the church, "this is Kate and I believe she is just who we need."

"That is good news," he sighed in relief. Turning to the hill girl he added, "That is a load off of my mind. I hate to leave Ann alone with winter coming. Dear, let's take them over to the parsonage so Kate can see her room," he suggested.

"Effie, maybe you could bring her things over by tomorrow?" Ann asked.

"She hain't got much so we brought everything today," Effie said. "Hit is all out in the wagon. We knew ye would be anxious fer her to get started."

"Good," Ann agreed. "John wants to go fishing right away with Tom Matthews, so he can go tomorrow!"

Walking to the wagon Effie kept up a lively chatter and brought up the subject of Granny Shook.

"Our Bob says he saw old Granny out by the barn last night. He tried to ask what she wanted but he said she just flat disappeared. I shore am glad to have Kate gone. That old womern gives me nervous fits. But she won't dare bother the Preacher." Ann couldn't tell her that she had met up with her before.

After the Childers drove off, Ann took Kate by the hand and led her into the kitchen. "Come on, Kate, we'd better feed that hungry man or he will feel mistreated." Setting the table, Kate seemed to relax a little. Her dark eyes filled once, but Ann pretended not to notice. She did notice Kate's frayed high-top shoes and faded dress which was already getting snug.

"Ye seen my Pa?" the girl asked. "War he still mat at me?"

"He did seem angry, Kate," Ann admitted.

"Pa will never git over what I done," Kate cried, "but Ma hain't mad. What did Ma say, Mrs. Nilson?"

"Your mother said she would come to see you when the baby is born even if she has to walk." Ann hoped this would be of comfort to her. During the meal John commented on how good the pie was that Effie had brought. Eagerly Kate interrupted.

"She cain't hold a candle to Ma, or me nuther," she declared.

"Good, maybe you can teach me," Ann said. "I've never tasted anything as good as the pies and cakes these women make." She saw a warm glow spread over Kate's face, and felt a warmth in her own. If she was not careful she would turn into a real domestic yet. Her friends would laugh if they could see her struggling with a wood stove, or pulling up the heavy buckets of water from the porch cistern.

After supper they all sat on the porch and watched the sunset. About a hundred feet across the yard, their forest friends were enjoying some table scraps. Ann had saved some bread for a pet skunk that came every evening looking for a handout. Once, she held out food and the beautiful animal had padded over and taken it out of her hand. It was so dainty with its pointed face and little body with a long feathery tail. Ann wished she could have one for a pet, and thought how horrified Aunt Cora would be. Suddenly she realized that she had not missed her aunt, Bill, or Denver all day. Looking at Kate, she knew that she would have to enlist her aunt's help soon. Kate would need so much and there was no chance of receiving a baby shower here.

At bedtime she helped Kate adjust to her first night in this strange house. Kate was awed by the striped, store-bought sheets and the downy comforter. She was used to sheets of bleached feed sacks and quilts heavy with toesacks and wool blocks. Ann had done her best to dress up the old iron bed and the cotton mattress.

"Thank ye, Mrs. Nilson," Kate said when Ann had tucked her in and was ready to blow out the lamp.

"Now why can't you just call me Ann? That would please me a lot. I hope we will be good friends. I don't have a sister and I feel you will be like one to me."

Kate gave her a warm smile. "I will think on it, and I shore hope I can earn my keep here with you and the Preacher."

After breakfast the next morning, John took his knapsack and blanket and rode off on the mare. He was looking forward to trying his hand at fishing. He had always lived in a city, and had had no time for sports. The mare stirred the leaf covering on the forest floor as he rode along. He saw a covey of wild turkeys, which protested his invasion of their territory. He thought one would be great for eating, but knew he couldn't kill it, and Ann wouldn't know how to dress or cook it.

After an hour, he came in sight of the Matthew cabin. John noted with surprise that it had once been painted red. Tom must not own a hound since no sound broke the morning quiet. As soon as John rode into the clearing, Tom was out to meet him.

"Hi, Preacher," he called, "you're just in time to join me for a morning snack."

"Ann gave me breakfast," John replied, "but I'll take a cup of coffee. This air gets sharper every day. Winter will be here before I'm ready. They say it gets real cold about Christmas."

"Yes sir, you can count on it. Some days it don't thaw at all. I've seen most of the creek iced up, and you can ride clear across the lake at the store in Gentry." Tom held open the door to the warm kitchen, where a large, raw-boned woman stood by the stove. "Preacher Nilson, this is Ma. She's got some good cobbler, so sit down and we'll fill up before we hit the trail."

"I'm glad to meet ye, Preacher," the hill woman said as John sat down. "If'n we had a wagon I'd be coming to meetings, but I jest cain't set thet old mule of Tom's." Mrs. Matthews looked at her son reproachfully. She was stout and her face was flushed from the hot stove. Her red hair was streaked with grey and styled in a bun on top of her head. She also wore a long apron as did all of the hill women.

"That surely smells good," John told her as he sat down.

"Tain't much," Tom's mother replied. "I jest use most any berries. This here is blueberry that I picked down by the creek. There ain't very much anymore cause bears love them too."

The kitchen was sparsely furnished, but John saw a shelf in the corner full of books. "It looks like you read a lot of books, Tom," he observed.

"Most of them was his Pa's," Mrs. Matthews said. "Tom don't seem to take much to them. His Pa was an engineer in these parts a'fore he got killed. Tom was just a little feller then. He's right set on going on to school. Jest like his Pa, Tom be. Sets more store on books than on plowing." Her querulous voice struck a strident note in the warm kitchen.

"Now, Ma, don't worry the preacher about me, he came up here to forget his troubles. That sun is climbing so we had better go. Say, Preacher did you bring a bedroll so we can stay out?"

"I brought one blanket. Will that be enough?" John asked.

"It will if you know how to bed down," Tom laughed. "I forgot you are a city fellow. Ma, don't look for me 'til you see me coming. We may just stay out all night."

As they rode along Burnt Creek, Tom pointed out every tall pine and every bend in the stream. Slowly they followed the swift, clear stream, stopping at each deep pool under the canopy of pines. Breathing in the clear mountain air, John burst into song, "Glory, glory, hallelujah!" The startled mare almost stumbled into the creek. Tom turned back and grinned broadly.

"Kind of gets you don't it sir?" he stated. "I always feel real happy when I ride along here. See that over there?" pointing to a clump of growth. "That is sangroot. Folks around here put a lot of faith in that herb. It is supposed to make you into a real he-man. I guess it might be better at that than some of the conjures these people practice."

John wondered what Tom meant but he did not ask. "Yes, lots of good things seem to grow wild here. I have heard a lot about sassafras."

"Now that is one I don't like," Tom admitted.

When they came into the open they could look down at the Matthews cabin nestled in its clearing with pines all around. Further along, the creek's deep pools reflected overhanging trees, vines, and rushes. There the wary trout waited in their shadowy holes. Sometimes they rode in near-darkness beneath towering sycamores and birches, then out into the golden sunlight. At first, John thought this a solitary place, but when Tom pointed out the squirrels, rabbits, and a grey fox on the far bank, he knew it was not.

Finally Tom stopped by a waterfall and a large pool. Standing on the bank away from the sun, he showed John how to cast into the boiling flood. John's first try was a disaster. His line caught in a tree, he lost his fly and broke his line.

"Don't mind, I have plenty more," Tom assured him. "I make them on long evenings when I run out of reading material. Here, try this one with duck down on it."

John finally got the hang of it and was amazed by an immediate tug on his line. Reeling it in under Tom's directions, he was rewarded with a glistening trout. As it flopped on the mossy bank, Tom came over and helped John retrieve the hook.

"Now of course you don't dare hold a catfish like this," he warned, "or you'll really get speared. This is a beauty. Looks like a two-pounder. This will be enough for our supper."

John felt anew the beauty of God's creation. He thought of

the smoke-filled city and of the many people who would never see a sight like this beautiful creek. He could not believe they had been here all afternoon. Tom built a small fire, and put on a pot of water for coffee. He showed John how to scale and clean the trout, then he rolled it in cornmeal and salt and laid it in his old iron skillet on the coals. John's mouth began watering when the tantalizing aroma filled the air. His cold sandwiches were forgotten as they feasted on the sloping bank of the creek, cushioned with leaves and moss. Afterwards they talked like old friends, soothed by the intimacy of the woods.

"Preacher, what do you reckon man was put here for anyway?" Tom asked.

"Each man has a job to do, Tom," John answered. "Sometimes it takes awhile for us to know Just what it is. Now take me. I was over halfway through college before I knew I had to be a preacher. Have you ever had any deep feelings about any one thing?"

"Only about what Pa did, but I don't want to do that. The books he left seem dull to me. I did think I should work the farm for Ma and trap for extra money, but I hate to kill and skin those beautiful creatures."

"I believe the best thing for you is to continue your schooling. Maybe the right choice will come to you as it did to me. How far have you gone in school?" John asked.

"I went three years to Siloam Springs College. I worked as a janitor for my board and room. Ma says we don't have enough money left to finish, and she needs me at home. She don't believe I need any more book learning," he concluded.

"That is a shame, Tom. A man can't get too much learning. There ought to be some way for you to be able to finish. Didn't your father have insurance?"

"Ma said he had a little, but it's all gone. She wants me to stay here and farm this place her folks left her. Guess that is why my father stayed on."

It seemed to John that all of the fun was gone from their trip. Then the young man's mood seemed to change. He jumped up, began to cut some branches, and piled them up.

"Got to get our sleeping room built before dark," he explained. "Help me pile up these leaves. You'll never believe how warm you'll sleep tonight."

"How about bears? Will they bother us?" John asked.

"I'll build up the fire through the night and they won't come near us. Besides, bears sleep at night and feed in the daytime. The most danger will be the coons and skunks after our grub. We'll stow it with us here."

John was amazed at how quickly Tom built the shelter. It was arranged like an indian tepee, and tied together at the top with vines. With his blanket on a pile of leaves, he was nice and warm.

"Come winter," Tom explained, "when I have to go out checking trap lines, I sleep like the indians: I dig a trench and fill it with coals, then I cover them with six inches of dirt, and put my bedroll on top. I can sleep warmly all night and never know it is freezing. Last winter I trapped clear up on Sawtooth. Sure are pretty fox and possum up there. I don't like it up there much. Folks say it's haunted, but I have never seen a ghost."

After settling in for the night, John saw an occasional star through the boughs. Once he heard a shrill whistle.

"That's deer coming down for a drink in the pool where we fished," Tom explained. "Guess you didn't see their trail down the mountain. Some men hide in the trees around here to get their kill. I think that is mean. The poor things can't get their scent in time to run."

"But Tom, the deer was put here for man to have for food," John argued.

"I know you are right, Preacher, but it still galls me. I've gotten out of fall butchering so far by being away at school, but I guess this year I'll have to do it. Ma's been after me already to kill her hogs so we can have lard and bacon. I guess everybody has problems, even you, Preacher. What bothers you?"

"Yes, Tom, even me. But I can only confide in God. I pray each day for someone dear to me." Suddenly John felt weary, and it was then off in the shadowy brush he heard a strange laugh… "Heh, heh, heh." He looked around at Tom but his body outline was quiet. Then it came again… "Heh, heh, heh." Sitting up, he asked Tom if he had heard it.

"Heard what?" Tom answered. "All I hear is the forest settling down."

"Well, I must have imagined it," John evaded. He wished he could unload his worries on this nice boy, but he knew he could not. Only God could know how he worried over Ann. The rigors of the life here were so hard on her. He was banking on Kate, and that by helping her, Ann would be more content. He tried not to let her know that he worried and that he knew about her former lover, Bill. Breaking off his unhappy thoughts, he turned back to Tom's problem.

"Why don't you try and go back to school, Tom? I'm sure we can find help for your mother. Maybe I can learn how to butcher," John suggested.

"The trouble would be the money. I'm past twenty-one now and there is no more free tuition."

"I'm sure I can help," John promised. "Tell you what, I'll write to Little Rock and see what I can find out."

"I'd sure like that, but don't say anything to Ma about it yet," Tom warned.

Wrapped in his blanket listening to the hooting of owls and the rhythm of the creek, John's mind went in circles as he tried to think of a way to help this fine, young man. He was so wise in the ways of the hills, but so ignorant of the outside world. John knew it would take a small miracle, but hadn't he already been asking for miracles? Before falling asleep he wished that Ann was lying here beside him. She would have loved this trip. He hoped in time he could take her on a fishing trip. Lord, help me, he thought. Don't let me lose her, I just can't give up! He seemed to hear the strange laughter then sleep finally came.

⊰ Chapter Four ⊱

Kate took to parsonage life like a kitten to cream. In the first few days she had taken over most of the cooking and cleaning. Ann managed to keep her from heavy lifting. When the mornings grew colder and the rains came, Ann was thankful that the well was on the back porch. Someone had been right when they built the parsonage, for they must have known it would be occupied by a nervous, city girl.

John had written some letters for Tom. One went to the engineering department where Mr. Matthews had worked. Help had been found and, over Tom's mother's objections, he was returning to college. John loaned him a suitcase, a dictionary, and a fountain pen from his seminary days.

Tom was confused and shy at his first meeting with Kate.

"She is staying with us this winter. I plan some overnight trips up beyond the mill, and I can't leave Ann here alone. Kate will be company for Ann," John explained.

"I think I met you once before," Tom told her, as Kate stood aloof by the fireplace. "I helped at your Pa's barn-raising. But you were so little then that I would hardly know you now."

Kate blushed. "I remember you, Tom Matthews. You shore was the biggest eater at the table that day. Ma said you ate a whole loaf of her fresh bread." She laughed at the memory. Ann knew this was the first time she had seen her look happy. Then Kate added, "Pa was awful mad when he saw how much them men ate."

"Well, he got his barn up didn't he?" Tom pointed out. "I've heard your pa is a real ornery man. It's a wonder to me he got anybody to come!"

"Oh, Pa helps on all of the raisings. He says the good book says that be right."

"I'm glad to see you are helping the preacher and his wife, Kate. Now I better be going soon. I've got a ride with a drummer to Siloam, and I have to meet him at the store about noon."

"That is luck, Tom," John said. "I've got the mare hitched up, and I'll take you to Gentry. We need a few things anyway." Turning to Ann, his eyes grew wary. Looking into her face he wondered if she wished she was leaving too. Then in an ordinary tone he asked, "What do you need from Yancey's, dear?"

"Just see if I have a package," she answered. "There should be an answer from Aunt Cora by now." She thought of the long list she had mailed to her aunt and was eager to show Kate the pretty things she had never known.

"Well, goodbye then," Tom told Ann and Kate. "Guess I won't be seeing you folks again until Christmas." He climbed in the spring seat with John, and the girls watched them drive off.

Ann had been surprised at the contents of Kate's trunk. Inside, there was a tablecloth embroidered with a design of blue flowers, and pillowslips with wide crochet edging. Ann thought they were as nice as any in the Denver shops. At the bottom of the trunk was the pride of every mountain girl: a bridal ring, or wedding ring quilt. Done in bright colors, it was made in preparation for the wedding night. Kate's eyes filled when she held it.

"Guess I'll never have no call fer this now," she sighed.

"Of course you will, Kate. In time this will be like a bad dream," Ann reassured her.

"I purely hope so. I cain't hardly remember Tim's face. Thet war his name, Tim Smith, but I never did tell Pa. He'd never believe me and he'd have made a lot of trouble fer him. Miss Ann, I never knowed nobody like Tim. He was kind to me and told me I was purty. He run up on me first when I was egg hunting on the ridge. Ma wanted some guinea eggs to hatch under her old hen. She fancies them guineas. Pa don't hold much with thet, but he lets her. Tim was standing there looking at me before I knowed hit."

Ann thought that Smith was an old dodge but she said nothing as Kate went on.

"I tried to run off, honest I did, Miss Ann, but hit was jest too late. After, I never tried to run. He told me how purty my eyes were, how soft my hair and skin was, and it jest seemed so sweet to be there. He told me about the big city whar he lived and promised he'd take me to see them when his job was over here. I know now I never should of laid with him, but I thought he meant all them fine words. Now no good man will ever want me." Her thin shoulders shook with sobs.

Ann felt her anger rise. In a way she had been enticed by Bill the same way, and she had enjoyed it. She knew that he had had no intention of marriage either.

"Don't cry, Katie, don't cry. You were just an innocent child. Time will heal this and now you have to think about your baby. Don't worry about finding a good man. I'm sure there is one waiting out there for you." Ann thought how lucky she was to have John and not a baby.

"I purely hope so," Kate responded doubtfully.

Before John was fully prepared, winter was upon them in its fury. He had nailed down the loose boards on the old shed for the mare; put several bales of hay under the lean-to; filled the crib with unshucked corn; and stacked cordwood close to the church building, assuring them warmth during services. Ann had jars of canned food stored on her pantry shelves. Lacking a cellar, they had a barrel of apples, turnips, and carrots in the back room covered with straw. The worst problem was the outhouse, which was almost impossible to reach on bad days. Ann soon learned the use of a "jar". John had carted their hens over to Hattie's for the winter. Next year he would build a place for them, and also for a cow. On the dark, winter days Ann was happy to have Kate's company. When her body began to swell, Ann decided to consult with Hattie.

She does not even know when this baby is due. What will we do if it comes unexpectedly? Shouldn't she go to Siloam and be examined by a doctor? Ann worried about something going wrong and she might be alone with Kate.

"Now don't ye fret, Mrs. Nilson," Hattie said. "Kate looks healthy to me. The little gals usually have the easiest time. It's them big heifers that lay fer hours. Jest send the preacher over soon as Kate's water breaks, and I'll be at your place in an hour. Have plenty of hot water and get some clean rags. Ye was a good helper up at the Wilks'. They don't many have sech a hard time as poor Jennie with little John."

Ann worried just the same. What if John was gone on one of his trips, then what would she do? What kind of a life had she gotten into? She wished she was back in Denver. Then John's loving face flashed in her mind, and she knew she would stick it out, whatever happened.

After the middle of December, Ann would not let John go on any long trips. She and Kate had been working on a few gifts for the children. Ann showed her how to make popcorn balls and strings. She had also written her aunt for hard candies, a box of oranges, and at least one store-bought present for the small children. Luke's sisters, and the Neeley girls had never owned a doll. The men seemed able to stay in snuff and chaw, but Christmas always found them too poor to buy anything for their children. The store in Gentry had dolls and if a family traded enough they were given one if they paid up. But most never got out of debt to Yancey. Ann longed for dolls with real hair and sleepy eyes. So she wrote her aunt to draw enough money from her account still left in the Denver bank.

Almost everyone now had a good word for the preacher. After they had taken Katie in most of the families had approved. Of course a few still sided with old Eli, some talked of Granny and what she might do, and that it was not the preacher's place to take in a girl like Kate. Ann knew that Hattie and Jess had held up for them on several occasions. Hattie was a part of their lives and many depended on her in time of trouble. And because of this, they had been accepted.

She wondered where old Granny was now, and what she planned to do to Kate. For her part she loved to have Kate to fuss over. Ann was eagerly looking forward to the baby. She had dreamed of one of her own some day... but not here in this God-forsaken place!

⚜ Chapter Five ⚜

The day of the first big freeze dawned like any other morning. John had banked the fire the night before so this morning there were still enough coals to start a new fire. He stood shivering within the warmth of the fireplace for awhile before going out to the kitchen to fire up the stove. Needing some wood, John started out the back door but found he could not get it open. As far as he could remember, there had never been a key to any of the doors so it could not be locked. After tugging awhile he decided to go out the front door. He could not get it open either. In frustration he called to Ann.

"There must be something blocking them," she told him. Looking out of the window she saw snow drifted high. "John, why don't you just go out of the window and clear the snow off?" she suggested.

"It won't budge either," he told her grimly.

"Ye might as well save all the trouble, Miss Ann," Kate informed them as she stood by her door in her flannel gown.

"Thet winder is going to need lots of hot water. Looks like we got us a good'un last night. Did you all hear the wind howling?"

"I sure did," Ann said as she checked the hot water reservoir on the side of the old cookstove.

"Kate, do you mean that our doors and windows are frozen shut?" John inquired in surprise.

"Shore do," Kate laughed. "Guess this be yore first freeze, so ye might as well get used to hit. We may not get no real thaw now a'fore spring. Most folks jest pick out the winder closest to the fire and use hit all winter. We used the one by Ma's cookstove at home."

Ann looked at the small window by their fireplace and wondered how Kate could squeeze through it later. "John, you'll have to put a step outside for us. I guess we could do it, but surely it won't stay this cold."

"Thar be some days warmer, and the door may thaw out after the fire's been on all day," Kate told them.

John wondered if the church door was frozen too. As soon as he could get out, he walked over to check. To his surprise, it opened. He reasoned it was because the morning sun shone directly on it. He decided to put wood in the big stove since they would be working there all day, and then he would go to Gentry to see if Ann's packages had arrived. After breakfast he asked Ann and Kate if they wanted anything from Yancey's store.

"You can bring me an inside toilet," Ann smirked. She missed her bath more than anything else in this God-forsaken place. Then seeing the hurt clouding John's kind face, she hurriedly added, "All I need are some licorice drops. Not for me, John, but for Jennie's little girls. I think Yancey's has them."

"You are going to spoil these children," John told her. "There won't be anything left for next year." *If there even is a next year* he thought.

During the long afternoon Kate and Ann made flannel diapers for the baby. They hemmed them and then made bands, which Ann did not fully understand, but Hattie had maintained were very necessary. Looking at the pitifully small collection of clothing, Ann thought of the fancy baby showers she had attended in Denver. Those expensive satin-bound blankets and lovely dresses were not for this unwanted baby. What Kate did not know about could not be missed. She wished Kate could have some of the crocheted items she had seen around the hollows here.

Late in the afternoon gray snow clouds rolled in again and Ann began to worry about John. The day matched her mood and she longed for just one bright electric light. As she brought in a heavy load of wood, she wondered how this preacher could have such a hold on her. Then, as a reprieve, she heard the creak of a wagon on the trail. Straining to see against the gloom, she made out two figures.

"Oh Katie, let's clean up this mess, it looks like we have company," Ann exclaimed.

"Who is it, Miss Ann?" Kate asked as she ran to the window. "Miss Ann, it be Tom Matthews and I shore do look a sight!" She rushed to her room smoothing her hair.

Ann watched the girl in surprise. At least she was getting over her hopelessness and was conscious of others. Picking up their sewing scraps, Ann hurriedly put on a pot of coffee and slipped a pan of raised bread in the stove. Ann also smoothed her hair and slipped into a clean apron. She had learned the beauty and convenience of aprons since living here. Soon she heard the two men stomping snow off their boots on the back porch. A gust of cold air preceded them into the warm kitchen. Both were carrying packages.

"Well, Ann, it looks like Santa will make it after all," John told her with a big grin. "Your aunt must have paid a lot of postage on this stuff. It's a good thing I had Tom to help me load the wagon."

"It is so nice you could get home for Christmas, Tom," she greeted the young man. "You don't look the same. The big city has changed you already."

"Siloam Springs is not very big," Tom protested. "I have been so busy studying and working that I didn't see much of it."

Ann could hardly wait to open the boxes, but needed to put something to eat out first. When Kate finally came out of the bedroom she had changed her dress and dusted her face with some powder Ann had given her. She also caught the interested looks Tom gave her. She felt as if she had contrived this meeting.

"Tom, you and your mother must come to our little program on Friday night," John invited. "You can take the wagon home with you now so it will be handy to bring her."

"Say, that would be right nice, Preacher. I'll make Ma come. It will do her good to get out and see folks for a change. I had a letter from her a few days ago and she seemed to be getting along pretty well."

"Yes, I saw her about a week ago when I took up things from the store. People beyond the mill had hauled wood for her, and she had had the hog slaughtered and dressed. She said she was looking forward to having you home for the holidays," John informed him.

Ann and Kate were excitedly looking over the contents of the boxes from Denver. Ann was grateful to her aunt. Even though she highly disapproved of her niece's lifestyle, she was always ready to help. Included were some sleepy-eyed dolls and some ivory-handled knives. She saw the faint furrow in John's brow.

"These things must have cost a fortune, Ann," he said. "Your aunt must have had to use some of her own money."

"Aunt Cora only wants me to be happy. She has always let me do about anything I pleased," she told him. "Come on Kate, let's open this last box."

"Nothing can best them dolls," the hill girl told her, caressing the hair of the one she was holding.

"Now, Katie, it won't be long until you can hold your very own real, live doll," Ann promised her.

The last box did not contain Christmas gifts. Among the tissue paper there was a dainty little dress, a pair of tiny satin shoes, and a small silver spoon. Kate had never seen such finery in all of her life. A look of bewilderment crossed her face as she gingerly touched the lace on the little dress.

"Miss Ann, did ye ever see such a sight in all yer borned days?" she whispered, her dark eyes shining.

"This is more than I ever thought we'd have for your baby," Ann admitted. "Won't it be nice to put these lovely clothes on it? I'm getting as excited as if this baby was mine." Ann saw the interest on Tom's face and began to have a secret hope for Kate.

When the bread finished baking, Ann set out the simple meal. Her red tablecloth made the rough pine room look bright and cheery. The way Tom ate the hot bread convinced her that it was still his favorite food. The evening brought more snow, so they urged Tom to stay.

"In the morning you can take the wagon. I won't be needing it now until after Christmas," John explained.

"That's nice of you, Preacher," Tom agreed. "I'll stay. Ma don't know when to expect me anyway. If I have the wagon she won't have an excuse not to come to the program Friday."

After dinner they sat by the fireplace and talked about the past months and of John's work. Ann saw Tom glance worriedly at Kate several times and wondered what he was thinking. She felt sure there was an attraction there. It is too bad these two did not meet before Kate's tragic experience, Ann thought, but perhaps it was not too late.

Turning her mind to the coming program, Ann needed to pick the right doll for each little girl. What a change she was feeling. After the grand parties of Denver, the lavish gowns, the elaborate gifts, and the gourmet food, what made her so excited here? What a silly fool she had become. Catching John's eye, she prayed he could not tell what she was thinking.

Early the next morning Tom and John hitched the mare to the spring wagon. Ann made coffee and wrapped a generous piece of bread for Tom to eat along the way. When John walked out to say goodbye, Tom said what had been on his mind the evening before.

"I want to thank you and Miss Ann for doing what you are for Kate. It makes me boil to think how Old Man Tate has treated her. Someone should teach that old reprobate a lesson, I sure would like to be the one too!"

"Now Tom, you know we are glad to have Kate stay here with us. I didn't know you felt so strongly about Kate," he probed, looking full in Tom's face.

"I didn't either, Preacher. Somehow I feel real sorry for her. It's a good thing that I don't know who that city fellow is, cause I'd make him think twice before he ever did a thing like that again," Tom vowed.

"And I'd help you," John agreed. "But now we'll just have to be kind to Katie and help her pick up her life again."

Tom nodded his head in solemn assent and John knew he was really interested in the little hill girl.

Watching him drive down the lane, John could see the wagon wheels sink into the fresh snow. Tom would be alright as soon as he reached the main trail. Another snow like this could make it very hard for the people to get to the church the next evening.

Ann and Kate tagged dolls and other gifts all that day. Kate cut out Christmas bags while Ann sewed them up. John was pressed into helping. By evening they were ready to be taken over to the church.

On Thursday the girls baked pies and cookies. Ann had never

tasted such a velvety, crisp pie crust as Kate's. Using fruit given to Ann, they made what John thought would be enough to feed an army. But Kate told them she had seen some men eat two whole pies and drink a gallon of coffee by themselves. Ann still could not understand her excitement. Nothing, except for the debutante dance when she had shown Bill to all of her envious girlfriends, had seemed this exciting. What was happening to her? Her thoughts were interrupted by John.

"I hope it doesn't snow again tonight. It would be a shame if people can't get here."

"Ye don't need to fret about that," Kate laughed. "Jest nobody'll miss the Christmas program. Why, they had it here last year and there war no preacher even. Jess and Hattie sort of jest took over. Jess brung his fiddle and, after eating, everybody squared. Guess Preacher might not like that though," she added, looking at John uncertainly.

"I had singing carols in mind," John admitted. "I'm sure that would be better on this occasion."

"Did they have any presents last year?" Ann asked.

"Oh yes, they all got something," Kate replied. "Everybody brings something and puts it in the barrels. One barrel fer the women, the other fer the menfolks. It's jest homemade things, but it's a lot of fun to draw out'n thet barrel."

"How wonderful," Ann agreed. "What did you get?"

"I didn't get to go, Miss Ann. Pa don't hold with much laughing and funning. But Lettie May, she told me all about hit. She said hit was the best time she ever had. But I heared she be making eyes at Tad Price from up at the mill."

"John, we must fix those barrels the same way this year," Ann declared. "I saw them in the storeroom."

"Sounds good to me," John agreed.

Searching through her trunk and dresser, Ann found a bottle of unopened toilet water that would do fine for her gift. But finding something for John was more difficult. Nothing she found of his was new. At last she found some fishing line and hooks he had bought in the fall at Yancey's store.

"Would you care if I used these?" she asked him.

"Sure, dear, go ahead," he agreed. "Sure beats giving them a tie, like I used to get."

Not this year, Ann thought. No room here for either ties, formals, or fancy clothes. Looking at her rough hands resignedly, she felt a sudden anger at her predicament. Granny Shook was right… this place was not the life for them. As soon as the holidays were past she would talk to John. Maybe it was not too late to get a church around Denver.

"I got some pink ribbon, Miss Ann. Hit was with that flannel yer auntie sent," Kate interrupted Ann's reverie. "Do you think I could use hit?"

"Well, now, it looks like we have taken care of the gifts," John laughed. "If you girls will stop and make supper, I'll go bring in some wood. We might as well wait until tomorrow to take these things to the church. It looks like it might rain and hopefully melt some of this snow."

"Hit ain't going ter make no never mind, Preacher. They'll come jest the same," Kate assured him.

That evening they practiced singing Christmas carols in front of the fireplace. Outside Ann could hear the whine of the wind, and occasionally a gust would come down the chimney and scatter the ashes. The eerie sound made her look up at the window where she expected to see the evil face of the old granny woman.

During the night Ann awoke to the sound of rain and the howling of wolves. In the warm bed pressed close to John, she shivered and was frightened. Could something happen to her because of her deception. All of these people, and even John, thought she was so good. Somehow she knew that John's God knew. She wished she could be better. Finally she fell into a troubled sleep.

The morning light roused John to find the doors and windows frozen shut. After firing up the cookstove, he waited quite awhile before the water was hot enough to use on the window. Climbing out he gave a low whistle of surprise.

"Girls, come take a look," he called.

Leaning out the window, Ann and Kate saw a sparkling, icy world. The trees were bent with loads of icicles and the back porch was fringed with them.

"Ye'd best be careful, Preacher," Kate cautioned. "This here be a good day to break yer bones. Ye had best take a bucket of ashes and spread them on the path a'fore ye."

"That sounds sensible to me, Kate. Guess you've seen this happen before," John agreed.

Kate handed him the bucket of ashes and he spread them about halfway to the church. He went back for a refill, and this time made it to the church. After breakfast, he swept out the church in preparation for the evening activities. Looking out over the rough pews from his pulpit, he could visualize the faces of those who usually sat in each one. Hattie and Jess always sat in the right front one. Each family had their own place, and if they were absent, no one else sat in their pew.

"Lord," he prayed, "let me be a light to these folk. Help me to teach them Your ways, and help them live happier lives. Help me to inspire their children to improve with a better education. Help me to show the older ones that it is better to love than to hate. Help me to learn their ways, so I can better understand them. And, Lord, help Eli to get over his hate for Katie, and especially help Ann to be happy here. Let her forget things from the past. Amen."

His heart felt lighter as he stepped down and began to rearrange the benches and pews along the walls. He found the two barrels in the back room, filled the kindling box, and cleaned out the pot-bellied stove. Then, he carefully built a fire to light later in the afternoon.

It was noon when John noticed a wagon drive into the yard. The wheels crackled as they cut ruts in the snow and ice. Going to the porch, John saw one of Rice Latham's boys, Jud, unloading a large blue spruce.

"Hi, Preacher," the boy called. "Pa sent me over with this here tree. We cut it yesterday on Sawtooth. Should've brung it sooner, but it froze up our way too. Pa said you'd need it."

"I hadn't even thought of a Christmas tree," John admitted. "I am glad someone did. The children would have been disappointed. Are your folks going to be here tonight, Jud?"

"They shore wouldn't miss hit, Preacher. I done whittled me a bald eagle with spread wings to put in that there barrel," he said in a voice full of pride.

"Well, I'll be looking forward to seeing that. Tell your father I thank him for sending us this beautiful tree," John called as the boy drove off.

Ann could scarcely believe her eyes when John brought her over to see the spruce. He made a stand and Ann covered the base with a sheet. Together, Ann and Kate strung holly berries and popcorn and placed them around the tree. At dusk they brought over the gifts and hid them under a table, carefully covered the pies and cookies with a snowy cloth, and John brought out the carol songbooks.

"Jest you wait, Miss Ann," Kate promised, "thet old moon will shine tonight. Hit will be so purty hit will jest near hurt yer eyes. Lots of folks will be coming. I wonder if Tom's Ma will be here?"

Ann had been wondering about that too, but had decided not to mention it. Soon they heard the creak of wagons and the sounds of people greeting each other. The air was so still every sound echoed back across the hollow. John held Kate's arm tightly, and Ann walked behind them on the cinder path. The hitching rail was lined with mounts and wagons and there were mules tied to every tree.

"Ann," John told her, "look at all of the strangers in there. Maybe we can get more acquainted tonight."

Ann was thinking that she had met enough of these hill people, but she did have to admit she was fond of the children. She saw Jennie and little John sitting along the wall and hurried over to greet them.

"Jennie, how the baby has grown," she exclaimed.

"I guess he had. Hit be nigh onto four months. He be a right good young'un. Guess he ort to be after naming him after the Preacher," and Jennie smiled.

"He is so sweet," Ann replied. "I wonder if I will ever have one like him."

"Wal, hit looks like ter me ye may jest git one soon," Jennie replied, looking over at Kate. "Hain't thet there Tom Matthews she be talking to?"

"It sure is," Ann answered in surprise. She thought it did not take them long to get together. Looking around the crowded room, she saw others were also watching their conversation.

"I'll bet his ma is fit ter be tied," Jennie observed. "She's all ways been set on things being jest so... she shore hain't going ter take to his liking Kate."

"Now, Jennie, let's not say anything yet. Where are Will and Luke? Didn't Will bring you?"

"Will air jest outside sampling somebody's old corn likker," Jennie sighed.

John walked to his pulpit and rapped for attention, interrupting Ann's reply.

"If everyone will take a seat, we will start our program. Bud, will you call outside and tell everyone that we are ready to start? First, we will sing a few carols. This is a wonderful occasion we are celebrating. Christ was born as a little baby, free of guilt. He grew up to endure shame and death for us all."

Ann's thoughts flew to Kate and her baby. It would certainly be born in shame, and have a cross to bear. These hicks were just as bad as some of the people she knew in Denver, waiting to pounce on anyone who strayed from their code of behavior.

Soon the little church was ringing with "It Came Upon A Midnight Clear" and "Silent Night". Ann imagined hearing the bells on the sheep as the shepherds kept watch. Lettie May was playing the pump organ better than usual. Ann looked at John, noticing how the lamps shone on his fair head. He was so different from the dark, good looks of Bill.

As the children recited their little verses she saw the proud looks on the rough faces of the hill men. Love is the same everywhere, but why couldn't they show it? Most of them were so shiftless that all they did was hunt and get drunk. If the women didn't work, they would all starve.

Soon, the program was over and Bud Childers walked up to the front by the pulpit. "I heered a noise outside, and I'll jest bet old Santy Clause is waiting ter git in!" he called out.

Ann looked at John in surprise. Why hadn't she known there would be a Santa? From the look on his face, John hadn't known either. The air was tense as the back door opened and a Santa came in wearing a snowy beard, stocking cap, and red flannel shirt. Someone had smuggled out the presents Aunt Cora had sent and Santa was passing them out. Ann felt a surge of indignation. Now everyone would think Santa had brought them. Berating herself as a hypocrite, she watched the little girls hold their new dolls close. When Santa got to the knives, there were loud exclamations of unbelief from the boys. Every mountain boy yearned for his own knife, but most had to wait until they were almost grown. Several carried knives that had been handed down from relatives.

John, seeing Ann's frown, slipped over and whispered, "Isn't this best, Ann? There's no need for anyone to know who bought these things. Santa will promise not to tell, and Tom and Kate won't either."

"You're right, John. Who cares who gets the credit?" But in her mind, she knew she cared.

Soon it was time for each person to march around the barrels and pick their present. Lettie May started playing a march on the organ and Hattie Meeks led the way. Everybody scrambled to get in line. Hattie was rewarded with a pair of knitted gloves. The array of homemade mufflers, handkerchiefs, rag dolls, embroidery, and crochet amazed Ann.

In the mens' barrel were knitted socks, gloves, fishing flies, duck and turkey callers, whittled horses, and the beautiful bald eagle Jud Latham carved. John hoped for the eagle, but picked a corncob pipe instead. Ann suppressed a laugh. She had fared better with a pretty cross-stitched sampler.

After the drawings, Bud started tuning up his fiddle and another man brought in his guitar. Everybody started clearing the benches.

"Ann," John whispered as he hurried her off alone, "do you think they intend to dance right here in the church?"

"It looks like it," she answered. "Why don't we just be quiet. What can it hurt? After all, you can't change people overnight!"

John winced at the sharpness in her voice. Was she saying his morals were wrong? For him the party was over. Then he felt Kate's hand on his arm.

"Preacher, I hope ye don't aim to cause no trouble. This here be the time for fun and they don't get much good times. One preacher got run clear off when he said they couldn't square in here. They don't mean no harm and who kin say hit be bad?"

"She is right, Preacher," Tom spoke up. "You have to bend a little if you intend on living up here."

"I guess so," John replied, "but it goes against all of my training. I think Ann and I will slip on out and go home."

"Kate and I want to stay and watch, Preacher," Tom said. "I'll bring Katie home later after I want to sample some of her pie."

John and Ann walked slowly back to the parsonage deep in thought. Both were glad to see Katie so happy. They had learned to love the shy, sweet girl. John had hoped that having her here would help ease Ann's loneliness. Had he married a girl unsuited to his work? He knew he loved Ann deeply and felt his prayers would prevail. Ann's voice broke into his worried mind.

"I wonder how Mrs. Matthews feels about Kate?"

"She probably won't think much of her. I have heard she considers almost everyone here white trash," John answered. "Right now I feel like that myself. Listen to that music... I believe they like to dance more than they like to hear me talk."

"Don't tell me you are feeling low!" Ann exclaimed. "Not my stalwart mountain man! Nothing has bothered you all of this time," she smiled. "Oh, I am sorry, John. That was a mean thing to say. But you take things too seriously. Let them dance. God knows they don't have much to be happy for in this forsaken place. You'll make it here, don't worry. Nobody could be more kind or helpful than you are."

"Of course you are right, dear, and I am so thankful to have such a wonderful wife like you to help me." In his mind he was praying silently that it would last.

Ann felt a warm glow as John held her close. In her way she was praying to love this place like he did. She thought about those she had grown to love... Kate, Tom, Hattie. John could look straight through her soul, never teased or hurt her, and she could trust him. So why did she keep thinking of the good times she used to have in Denver? The old hill woman's words filled her mind—"ye don't belong here, so git out!"

⇥ Chapter Six ⇤

As they sat by the fire in the parsonage, Ann and John could hear feet stomping and the melody of Bud's fiddle. Ann thought it must be fun to square dance and wished that they could have stayed. Soon, they heard the back door open and in came Kate and Tom. Kate looked flushed and excited.

"Preacher," Tom began hesitantly, "Katie and I want to talk to you and Ann."

"What is it, Tom?" John asked, wondering at the young man's serious manner.

"Well," Tom went on, "you know how bad it has been for Kate and it won't be any better when the baby comes. I've been thinking that she needs a good man to take care of her, and I want to be the one to do it. I've been talking to her, and she says she'll take me. We want you to marry us before the baby comes."

"Does this mean that you will drop out of school?" John asked in concern.

"No, Katie wants me to go back and she hopes you folks will let her stay on with you until my spring term is over. Then I'll find a summer job in Siloam Springs. Ma won't like it, but I feel I am old enough to make my own decision and I want to share my life with Kate. She could move into town where I could help look after her if it gets too hard for her to live up here."

"Kate, do you feel that Tom is the one you want to be the baby's father? You are young and there are a lot of years ahead for you," John asked.

"Why, Preacher, what a thing ter say! I be the luckiest girl in these here hills. I never seen a gooder man than Tom. He air a sight better to me than Pa ever was. Preacher, he sure believes in your God, and he done told me that nobody could be as kind as you less'n God done it." Kate's voice was firm with conviction.

Ann was thinking that this was a relief. She had grown to love the little hill girl, but did not want to raise her. What a break to get Tom with his dark, good looks. Any girl would be attracted to him. But she made a silent bet that all wouldn't be so great when Tom's mother heard about it. She heard John's kind voice giving his approval.

"You tell Mrs. Matthews your plans and Ann and I will do all we can for you."

Soon the music stopped and they heard people calling back and forth. "Guess I had better go get Ma and take her home," Tom said reluctantly. "Preacher, I'll bring your wagon back tomorrow. I'll talk with you more about this. Tonight I'll have a job trying to convince Ma." Tom went out the back door so he and Kate could say goodnight in private.

"I have been expecting this," John informed Ann. "Tom showed an interest in Katie the first time he saw her here."

"I noticed it too," Ann agreed. "She is one lucky girl! It's a shame she couldn't have met him first."

"Remember up here people grow up faster and get married younger. We must encourage Tom. I have a good feeling about him. I believe he has a special job to do."

At that moment the back screen slammed and they heard Tom calling, "Preacher, come here! Katie fell on the ice and I think she is hurt!"

John ran to the back door. Kate was sobbing in pain. Together John and Tom carried her inside to her bed. Her face was white and drawn with pain.

"She stumbled and fell on that damn ice," Tom explained. "She seemed to be frightened of something. Ann, do you think we better get Hattie?"

"Don't ye leave me, Tom," Kate cried. "She might come back. Don't let thet old woman in this cabin," she pleaded.

"What are you saying, Katie?" John questioned. "Who frightened you?"

"I know who she means," Ann told him, shivering. "She means Granny Shook. She must have been here tonight."

"Thet's her," Kate cried. "Don't ye let her in. I jest know something bad be coming if'n ye do." She doubled up in pain.

"John, I think Tom had better go for Hattie. Maybe if he unhitches the mare he can overtake them." Ann tried to speak calmly, but inside she felt a churning of fear. Please, God, don't let anything happen to this baby, she prayed. "Tom, hurry," she added urgently.

"Preacher, will you go bring Ma over here?" Tom's face was drawn with worry. "She sure won't like this one bit."

As John went out with Tom to unhitch the mare, Ann bathed Kate's face with a cold cloth and held her hand. She wanted to ask about Granny Shook, but decided to wait. Once, after Kate was limp from a hard contraction, she hurriedly put a bucket of water on the cookstove, put in more wood, and gathered all of the clean clothes she could find. She remembered the night at Jennie's. What if Hattie wasn't back in time? Maybe Mrs. Matthews had some experience in delivering babies. Her worry was interrupted by Kate's cry.

"Oh Miss Ann, hit be awful bad! That old womern said I had to pay. She tried to push me in the well. Tom war going ter git his Ma. He come back when I screamed. I wish Ma was here. Oh Miss Ann, what will I do?" She held Ann's hand so tight it hurt.

"Now Katie," Ann comforted, "we will take care of you. Granny Shook can't hurt you here. Tom will be back with Hattie soon. Maybe his mother will help too."

"Ye don't need to count on me," Tom's mother spoke from the door. "When a body makes his bed hard, tain't nothing left to do but lay in hit."

"Please, Mrs. Matthews," Ann remonstrated, "now is not the time to talk that way. Didn't you ever make a mistake in your life? Kate needs our help tonight."

"She shore seems to need my Tom, as everybody saw tonight," the angry woman complained. "A'flaunting herself in front of folks as big as ye please! And my poor Tom, he hain't got no better sense than ter fall fer hit. I told him, I did, not to expect me to take care of no young'un! I jest know she done something to conjure him," the woman added.

"Now Mrs. Matthews, come sit here by the fire and I will get you some hot coffee. Let me take your coat," Ann offered.

"Don't need nothing, and I'll jest keep my coat. I need to git on home, clear away from all of ye. I jest knowed that Tom wouldn't amount ter much. All he did was read them books. Now I ain't going to set here and see him make a fool of himself with thet Kate," she declared.

"We can't take you home until Tom returns," John answered. "And feeling as Tom does, I doubt if he will want to leave until he knows Kate is all right," he added.

The angry hill woman made no answer as John hurried to the bedroom. He knew by Kate's contorted face that her time was close. He went to the bed and took her clenched hand.

"Kate," he urged, "don't hold in so. If you want to cry out, go ahead. It will relieve your pain."

"I jest cain't," the suffering girl sobbed. "Not with her setting in there jest waiting to tell Tom what a coward I be. I ain't aiming to make hit no worse fer him than hit be now. But Miss Ann, I never knew hit would be this bad." Kate's hands gripped the brass bedrail over her head and she gritted her teeth to keep from crying out.

John paced back and forth between the bedroom door and the front window. This night must be like the night Mary of long ago gave birth. Could it have been as hard for her? He was shocked by the pain a woman must bear. He wondered if Ann could stand a birth like this. he hoped if it ever happened she would be close to a doctor. Tom had been gone long enough to be back, could Kate stand much more of this? Then he realized Tom would have had to follow Hattie home so she would also have a horse to ride.

Ann ran out of the bedroom in alarm. "John, I just don't know what to do," she cried. Walking over to Mrs. Matthews she asked, "Mrs. Matthews, did you ever help with a birth? Is there anything we could be doing for Kate?"

"Ye and the preacher ought to hev been thinking on this a'fore now. When ye go ter butting inter folkses' business, ye air looking fer trouble. The only birthing I was ever to war my own when Tom come. I know they fed me some likker, so maybe ye could try hit," she told them grudgingly. "Ye could go git the chopping ax and put hit under her bed."

Ann thought Tom's mother must be crazy when she mentioned an ax. But she remembered hearing a lot of superstitions since coming here. She heard John answering the hill woman.

"We don't believe in using spirits much, besides we don't keep them. But maybe Hattie will bring something with her when she comes."

"If she ever gets here," Ann cried and flew back to the bedroom as Kate cried out.

"Oh Miss Ann," the tormented girl sobbed, "I'm so scairt. I wish Ma could come. Where is Tom, please call Tom." Her words faded into a cry of pain. Ann felt she could not stand to see Kate's frail body tormented much longer.

"Tom will be here soon with Hattie. She will know how to help you. Try and think about how nice it will be to hold your own little baby," Ann comforted her.

"God ain't a'going to let me off thet easy, Miss Ann." Kate sobbed. "I jest know old Granny be right. They be going ter punish me jest like my Pa said."

As she held Kate's hand and murmured encouragements, Ann felt that this night would never end. Could Granny Shook have had anything to do with this? She felt a premonition of fear for Katie. She remembered the threat made against her and John. She wished they could leave this superstitious place.

John brought in hot coffee and they helped the weakened girl drink some. Tom's mother still sat in the rocker in front of the dancing fire and refused John's offer of coffee. John saw her slip something from her pocket up to her mouth. He realized that she, like so many women in the hills, was a snuff dipper. He remembered how Hattie had advocated its use, saying it preserved your teeth. John hated to see the tobacco juice trickle out of the corners of people's mouth when they spit.

John heard the horses first and was out the back door before Tom and Hattie could dismount. He helped Hattie down and hurried her into the house.

"We have been so worried, Mrs. Wilks," he said. "Kate seems to be having a very hard time and Ann is frightened. I'm sorry we did not know this was going to happen before you left church tonight."

"I been expecting hit," the plump little hill woman

answered. "Let's go and git this party over with. How's Tom's ma taking hit?"

"Not very well I'm afraid," John replied. "Katie is in the front bedroom," he told her needlessly as the girl's cry filled the cabin. Hattie hurried into the room and glanced at Mrs. Matthews who did not look up or speak. Closing the door, she asked Ann to hold the lamp while she examined Kate. Ann watched as she kneaded Kate's stomach, then slowly shook her head.

A cold chill came over Ann as she looked questioningly at Hattie. Was old Granny's threat coming true? Could she really put a hex on someone? Ann never let herself believe in witches.

"Hit shore looks like a breach baby ter me. Them's the worst kind, and with Kate so little and all. Git that bottle in my bag over there. This here young'un is going to take awhile and Kate cain't stand hit much longer. Go git me a cup of strong tea. That and a little moonshine ought to ease her some."

Tom came in from tending the horses. "How is she, Preacher?" he asked. "Did we make it in time? I sure pushed the mare." When John did not answer immediately he turned to his mother. Seeing the anger still in her face, he went to Kate's door and looked in. "Mrs. Wilks, is Kate all right?" Seeing her worried face, he turned to his mother again.

"Don't ye worry none, Tom. That young'un will git here soon enough, more's the pity. If ye think ye can take the time, why don't ye take me home? That fire needs to be banked or everything will be froze by sunup."

"Ma, I can't go off with Kate in such bad shape. Can't you wait a little longer?" Tom begged. His broad shoulders were bent with worry.

"Go ahead and take your mother home," John spoke up. "She is not doing any good by staying here. You can be back in a couple of hours."

Tom looked at the closed door and his face reflected his anxiety. "Preacher," he said, "if there only was a doctor here. I could ride for him. Surely there is one closer than Siloam Springs. If only there was something I could do for her!" Tom clenched his hands in despair.

"All we can do is wait, Tom, and pray," John assured him. "You know Hattie will take good care of her. She is as good as a lot of doctors at this kind of thing."

John hurried Tom out and together they brought out the wagon and the protesting mare. "Tom, if we keep praying for Katie, I'm sure she will do fine. In the meantime, treat your mother gently. I'm sure her anger will pass. Mothers just want the best for their children."

"I guess Ma has about given up on me," Tom sighed. "I just never did do to suit her and guess I never will. I can't be like Pa. I wish she had had more kids than just me. Then she might let me alone."

Watching the young man drive up the moonlit trail with his mother, John prayed silently that their problem would be resolved. He could teach Kate to speak properly, and take her place beside him in whatever work he chose. John felt Tom somehow was special, and would amount to something good. As he opened the screen door and entered the kitchen, he suddenly realized the quiet. Something was wrong. Hurrying to the bedroom, he met a white-faced and stricken Ann.

"Oh John, Kate's baby is dead," she said and fell sobbing into his arms. As he held her close to him, he wondered what this would mean to them. Was it better this way? What chance would the child have had in a place that would never let Tom forget?

"Don't cry, dear, maybe it is all for the best," John whispered to her.

"No, no," Ann protested. "I was counting on having this baby to love. How could God let a thing like this happen? Oh, John, that old woman caused her to fall. I hate her! I better not ever meet her again!"

"You know better than that," John remonstrated sternly. "God knows what is best. Kate's child would have had a hard time growing up here." John felt troubled at her outburst.

"I don't care, it's not fair. The way poor Katie suffered and nothing to show!" Ann felt beaten by the tragedy.

Hattie came out of the bedroom looking grim. "Hit shore hurts me deep down to lose a young'un, Preacher," she cried, "but hit may be God's blessing this time."

"Is Kate going to be alright?" John asked anxiously.

"Shore hope so," Hattie replied soberly. "She be resting now, and if she stays quiet come morning, we'll have a better chance."

"Hattie, do you think the fall on the ice caused the trouble?" Ann inquired.

"Don't rightly know, Miss Ann. Don't many babies get their-selves so twisted up that way with the cord all around their neck. Most times they make hit through, but hit shore be hard on the womern. Maybe if she'd a had a doctor he could have saved hit. God knows, I shore tried."

"Hattie, now don't go blaming yourself," Ann objected. "It could have been old Granny Shook's doing. We didn't tell you that she was around here tonight. She scared Katie and that's what caused her to fall."

"Dear God, ye don't say! Wal, if she be here hit shore were for no good. That old womern ain't nothing but pure trouble. Last I heerd she be up to the mill." Hattie looked nervously around.

The three sat by the fire thinking of what could have been and what should have been. John felt especially bad for Ann. The flames flickered feebly and John got up to put on another log. Hattie made countless trips to the bedroom to make sure Kate was breathing properly.

When Tom finally rode in, John met him in the kitchen. There he told him as gently as he could of the baby's death.

"Oh God," Tom cried, and put his head down on the table. Shaking his head he looked up at John with a puzzled face. "Why did it have to happen, Preacher? We wanted that baby. It was part of Kate. I didn't care about that other fellow. I know this wouldn't have happened if we could have had a doctor." Walking into the front room he confronted Hattie. "Do you think a doctor could have saved Kate's baby?"

"Shore might hev, Tom. Ye see, hit took jest too long a'borning and thet cord jest squeezed the breath out of it."

"Preacher, that's it!" His dark eyes flashed with excitement.

"What are you talking about, Tom?" John asked.

"That is what I am going to do with my life. I will be a doctor and I'll be one right here where folks need one." His hand gripped John's arm hard.

"But Tom, it will take years to get through that much schooling and you'll need a lot of money."

"Then I'll get a job. Ma and Kate can manage. It could be that Ma will help—she admitted last night that Pa left money for my education but she just didn't want me to go away. If she won't, it won't make any difference. I know I can find a job."

"If you really mean it, Tom, I'll help you. Kate can stay here until you are through at Siloam this spring, then we will get you registered in Little Rock for the next term. It won't be easy, Tom," John warned.

Ann saw the glow on Tom's face and felt an envy she had never known before. To feel a need and then be able to fill it must be wonderful. Still, she knew she was really needed by her sweet man.

Day was breaking when Hattie came out of the bedroom with a triumphant face. She told Ann to warm up some soup as her patient was hungry. Tom made a beeline for the bedroom. The others left them alone so he could comfort Kate in private.

"Hattie says for you to eat all of this," Ann ordered. "Katie, I'm so glad you are feeling better."

"I'll feed it to her, Miss Ann," Tom offered and took the bowl. "Kate feels it may be better this way. Some day we will have a baby of our own, and we'll have a doctor handy, you can bet."

"Don't ye feel bad, Miss Ann," Kate spoke. "Ye've been so kind ter me, I feel real bad fer ye. But the poor little thing would sure be looked down on around these hills. Miss Ann, it be a girl, and I wanted ter name her fer ye."

Glancing against her will at the cradle in the corner, she saw the covering of pink flannel. She felt such a great disappointment she could not speak. Not wanting to cry, she hurried out of the room.

That afternoon Tom and John built a little box of rough pine boards and Hattie dressed the baby in the beautiful dress from Aunt Cora. The baby was wrapped in the pink, flannel blanket with the satin binding and buried in the snowy ground at the old cemetery. Hattie waited until after the burial and then rode home on her old mule. As Ann watched her wind her way up the trail, she thought of how kind the mountain woman was. She wished she could be more like her.

⚜ Chapter Seven ⚜

Tom spent most of his time with Kate during the holidays. He would carry her to the big rocker by the fireplace where they would sit in quiet companionship. Mrs. Matthews came on Christmas to share dinner bringing pies and a stewed hen with dumplings. Ann thought she could detect a softening in her manner toward Tom and Kate.

As the time approached for Tom to leave, he seemed to be worried. "Preacher, Kate and I want to be married before I leave. The only thing is, I don't have a ring. Do we need one to make it legal?"

"That is the custom, Tom," John answered. "However, it is just as legal without one. Maybe we can find one for you to use until you can buy one."

"I'd feel better. I will talk to Ma tonight. I'll be leaving in a couple of days, and I'd rest a lot easier knowing Kate is my wife. She's a sweet girl and I sure don't want to lose her to some of these boys around here."

"I don't believe you have to worry," John smiled. "Kate seems real fond of you." Then in a more earnest tone he added, "I believe you will be a fine doctor some day, Tom."

"That is my goal, Preacher. It will take awhile, but I have made up my mind," he said decisively.

The next evening John married the couple in front of the parsonage fireplace. Ann stood beside Kate and held on to the trembling girl. To everyone's disappointment, Mrs. Matthews chose not to come. But she did loan Tom her gold band to use until he could get a ring for Kate. She told him that if he wanted to tie himself down, she wouldn't stand in his way.

The young man departed the next morning, promising to write Katie and his mother every week. Ann felt happy and tried to forget the threats of old Granny Shook. The morning sun felt so good, and she vowed to try and make John happy.

The next few weeks were so cold services on Sunday mornings were sparsely attended. Ann couldn't blame people—it was hard to ride in the open wagons. At the end of February John said they needed to get out, so they bundled up warmly for the ride to the winter social in Gentry. The cold was not bad riding on a bed of straw down behind the spring seat. John had to face the cold wind.

It was dusk when they arrived, and wagons and mules were thick around the schoolhouse. Inside, people were grouped around the huge fireplace at the end of the room. The Childers were there, and the Wilks were also, as Ann saw Lettie May talking with some young man that she did not recognize.

"Hi, Mrs. Nilson," Lettie greeted her as she approached with her young man. "This here be Tad Price. He lives up Burnt Creek and his pa runs the mill on Sawtooth. Guess you and Preacher hain't been that fur yet. Tad, this here is Kate. She be living at the preacher's fer awhile. Reckon as how you be living in the big city soon?" she asked Kate.

"I shore will," Kate answered with a smile. "When Tom comes home this spring, reckon I'll go up to his place."

"I sat your ma awhile back," Lettie began. "She shore looked bad when we told her about the baby."

"Does she know me and Tom be married?" Kate asked.

"No, don't reckon so. We'uns jest heard it tonight from Yancey when Pa stopped at the store. Your Ma, she's been right sick," Lettie continued. "Pa says she's took bad with rheumatiz and can hardly walk."

"Oh, how awful," Ann said. "We will have to go see her Kate."

"I purely would love to go if ye think Pa will let us see her," Kate answered.

Soon, lines formed and Ann watched in amazement as a loud-mouthed man led the dancers through the patterns.

"I shore wish Tom be here," Kate spoke wistfully. "Did ye and the preacher ever square?"

"No," Ann replied, "but it looks like a lot of fun." She thought it was different from any dancing she had seen before but could not be as good as dancing cheek to cheek in the warmth of Bill's arms. Looking around the hall she saw John talking to someone she did not know. He looked like a blonde god next to these rough mountain folk, she thought. Some of the men did look nice in their store clothes, but most of the women were dowdy. Only the young girls wore their hair hanging loose. It seemed as soon as girls got married, they put their hair up in a bun. Ann intended to object if Katie did.

Soon the wife of the store owner came over to talk. Rose was thin and nervously fluttered her hands. Even her eyes darted around nervously. Her talent was spreading the news since she was in the best place to hear everything. The trouble was that she seemed to take great pleasure and satisfaction in twisting the facts around to make the telling more interesting. She reminded Ann of a blackbird shrilling an alarm over the least thing.

"Guess you know your Ma is ailing," she told Kate with an accusing air.

"Yes, we just heard about it tonight," Ann answered for Kate. "We hope to get over to see her next week."

"They say old Granny Shook is up there treating her. I'm surprised Eli let that old woman in his cabin," Rose added. "Eli sent to the store for poke root to make her some tea." She looked at Kate expectantly.

Kate hung her head and then looked helplessly at Ann.

"Thet shore don't sound like Pa," she admitted. "Granny is kin to Pa way back," she hastened to explain. "She may jest heered about Ma and come on her own hook."

Ann quickly turned Kate away and they found a seat along the wall and watched the dancers. She was aware of the curious glances turned their way. None of the young folk asked Kate to join in. Damned hypocrites, Ann thought. There wasn't one of them as sweet and good as Katie. Finally John came over and suggested that they should start for home.

As they left the hall they passed a group of older women and Ann heard one of them whisper "That's her. That there be the one old Granny said..." Ann could not catch the rest, but she noticed that Kate had heard. Damned hypocrites, she thought again. She would love to tell them off. Then she remembered that it would not be any way for a preacher's wife to act.

The next day it stormed. Ann knew they could not go see Lucy. During the afternoon Kate broached the subject of the womens' remarks.

"I don't rightly know jest what old Granny be talking about me fer," Kate reasoned. "I hain't hardly seen or heered tell of her since last Christmas here. I know she has powers, but Ma never did believe hit. And Pa never used to have much to do with her."

"What do you mean about her having powers? Is she a witch, Kate?" Ann queried nervously.

Laughing self-consciously, Kate replied, "We never did believe in sech things, but they be lots of folks around that hold to hit."

"But how can you tell if a person is a witch?" Ann pursued. "Did you ever know anyone who was?"

"Pa would switch me if he knew I told ye, Miss Ann. But I know ye ain't fixing to spread hit around. We got one womern up beyond the mill that worked a conjure once on the man she married. I don't know what she done else though."

"What do you mean, worked a conjure?" Ann demanded.

"Well, hits kind of like a charm. This womern wore a peach seed filled with some kind of stuff around her neck and my cousin saw her buying yellow garters at Gentry's store. Anyhow, she hooked old Buel Price, but they say he turned out no good. Later my Ma came up on her at her outhouse, a'saying the Lord's Prayer backwards, and that be a sure sign. Another old power womern got mad at Old Man Hawkins. She went over to his cabin to buy some setting eggs, and said he wanted to charge her way too much. She told him he would be sorry he tried to cheat her. And sure as ye be born, the next week, all of Hawkins' hens up and died fer no reason a'tall."

"That is unbelievable," Ann protested. "I have read about things like that, but I thought they were just old folk tales."

"Ye might be scared if ye knew some of the things that go on in these here hollers, Miss Ann," Kate went on. "Why up to Sawtooth mountain they say the spirits git together and a body jest better not be caught up there come night!"

Ann shuddered. "I won't ever go up there. I hope we can go to see your mother by tomorrow."

That night Ann told John about the witch tales she had heard from Kate. John had not been aware of any such stories. Most of the mountain people still looked on him as an outsider and had not confided much in him.

"You probably would not have heard much except for Katie," he told her. "She probably made it sound worse than it really is worrying about her mother. You know how people talk here. Anyway, we'll try and go over to the Tates' place tomorrow."

During the night Ann's dreams were invaded by foreboding fantasies. She awoke to a dreary morning, although it was not raining. John decided they should make the trip to the Tates. He didn't like the worry he saw on both girl's faces. They bundled up and started out before the mist had lifted from the valley.

"Hit shore be a cold'un today," Kate complained, as she huddled below the wagon seat.

"How long does winter last up here?" John asked.

"Mostly hit freezes clear up in May," Kate replied. "Once in June, Ma lost all her first planting. The fruit all froze cause most had jest set on."

Ann was affected by the cold and fog. Only the tops of the pine trees were visible above the mist. Without the sun, the world would be a dreary place, she thought. None of the usual wood creatures greeted them and the birds were in hiding. Smoke rose from several cabins. Ann knew the people were huddled around their fires. After two hours of bumping in the wagon, they topped a rise and could see the Tate cabin.

"At least they be home," Kate sighed in relief. The hound bayed a greeting. "Guess Pa felt like staying in. Wonder if old hound Molly still knows me?"

When they reached the yard Ann saw a curtain move and knew that their presence was known.

"You girls get down," John instructed them. "We might as well let Eli know that we intend to see Lucy." He tied the mare to the porch rail, then greeted the hound, who acted glad to see Kate. Joining the girls on the porch, he knocked loudly on the cabin door.

"What fer air ye doing here, and with her too?" Eli growled

as he opened the door. "Ye done hurt yer ma enough," he accused, glaring at the shaking girl. "Looks like ye'd be decent and let her be!"

"I don't understand, Mr. Tate," John interrupted. "Kate has not seen her mother for a long time."

Kate stood as one dumb under the onslaught of her father's rage. Seeing her white face, Ann put an arm around the girl. She felt like yelling back at the mean, old man, but knew that John would not like it. Eli's face had become livid, and he was hopping around on his short legs, reminding Ann of some of Hattie's banty roosters.

"She knows how she's been sinning agin us all," Eli thundered. "Now the Lord be punishing her ma fer not teaching her better. Hits her fault if her ma dies!" His sparse, white hair seemed to stand on end in his excitement.

"Mr. Tate, you must calm down," John admonished. "I'm sure the Lord is not punishing anyone. Katie loves her mother and wants to see her, no matter what you think."

"She hain't setting foot in this cabin," the old man declared. His face turned purple. "Granny told me to keep her and ye out."

"Is Granny a doctor?" John asked.

"She be a power doctor, Preacher," Kate told him quietly, darting a look at her father.

"Mind yer tongue, young womern," Eli warned her. "Hit be bad enough to take up with outsiders, but ye don't have to run off at the mouth too!"

"Pa, please let me in," Kate pleaded. "I do want ter see Ma fer a little."

Ann could stand it no longer, and pushed her way in the door. "Mr. Tate, you can't treat your sweet little daughter this way. She has had nothing to do with your wife's illness. So stand aside, because we are coming in."

"She done lost all claim to her home here," the old man roared. I jest want ter know whar thet baby she borned is at?"

"We buried Kate's baby in the cemetery the day after it died," John explained.

"Tain't what I heered," Eli answered. "Folks is saying she give hit away."

"That's a lie, Pa," Kate cried. "The little thing be born dead."

"Shore hit be borned dead, but that be why some would want hit," Eli went on, looking accusingly at Kate.

"Oh Pa, I never done sech a thing. You can jest ask the preacher here, 'cause him and Tom nailed her up in thet box, and took her right over and buried her. Miss Ann and me never went, it be so cold," Kate sobbed. When her father moved back a little from the door, she darted past him and ran to the bedroom. Lucy was cowering under the quilts.

"Ma, hits me, Kate! I come see how ye be. Is hit bad, Ma?"

Pulling the covers from her head, Lucy's white face filled with fear. "Don't ye stay here Kate. Go on back to the preacher's. Yer pa has lost his senses. He thinks I'm witched, and that ye be the cause of hit. I keep telling him hit ain't nothing but my old bones gitting rusted up, but he and Granny think you be having took with witchcraft. I know hit ain't so, but you better git out of here quick. There be no telling what he may take in his head to do. I'll be better come spring and hit be warm agin."

"I hope so Ma. I wish ye could know Tom. I got me the bestest man ever ye did see. Preacher Nilson married us before he left and now ye don't need to worry about me no more." Kneeling by the bed she kissed her face and held her mother close. "I'll come back Ma a'fore spring. If ye get bad, jest have somebody git word to the preacher and he'll bring me back."

Ann, watching from the door, saw the little woman smile at Kate. When they returned to the kitchen, Eli was sitting quietly under John's stern gaze. When he saw Kate his anger returned.

"I hope ye be finished fer good and all. Jest don't ye come around here no more. Yer Ma has took all she can stand account of ye. Jest fergit us from now on out," he shouted.

"We be going, Pa but I aim to come back and see Ma. I do wish Ma could get to a doctor. I hate to think she be laying in thet bed all winter." Kate faced him defiantly.

"Don't need no doctor," Eli growled. "All they want is yer money, and we shore ain't got none. Old Granny, she knows what ter do." Facing Kate and John, he held up a shaking finger. "She says ain't nothing going to help Lucy as long as we have anythin' to do with ye, so git!"

"We had better go," John decided, taking Kate and Ann by the arm. Turning to the old man he warned, "Eli you know your wife needs help. I would be glad to take her to Siloam. You must believe in God. Why don't we have prayer for her right now?"

"I kin do my own praying. I don't need no help from no shirt-tail preacher. The best thing ye can do is git on back across the holler and stay there!" Eli shut the cabin door and they heard the bar fall in place.

As they drove toward home John saw that Kate was crying. What could a man do in the face of such superstitions? "I am sure your father thinks he is right," he told Kate. "We must pray for Eli and have faith in God's power over evil."

"Praying may be fine," Kate agreed, "but all I know is that my ma be laying there and not able to git up. I never did think Pa would take up with old Granny that way."

"Sometimes misfortune will turn a man's mind until he doesn't know what to do. Eli's pride was hurt badly, Kate. Because of you his standing in the community is hurt too. So try to understand how he must feel. We should pray for him and your mother every day."

"Do you really think hit does good, Preacher? I mean praying so much. How do ye know God has time to listen to everyone?"

"I know he does, Katie. I can feel his presence. You must believe that God is real or you have nothing to stand on when trouble comes."

"I'll shore try and do hit," Kate promised. "I know my Tom believes in you. He thinks right smart of you, Preacher, and I do too." Her face brightened as she thought of Tom.

As they drove on John wondered what else he could have said to help ease Kate's heartache and how he could help the people in these hills. He knew that God and prayer had been his comforts since coming here. If only Ann could feel their power—but he knew she had not discovered his secret yet.

⚜ Chapter Eight ⚜

It was a week after the visit to the Tate cabin that Ann discovered a small wooden doll leaning against one of the log posts of the outhouse. It was a crudely carved image in a long flannel gown. Ann carried it back to the cabin, wondering who it belonged to. That night when she and John sat down for supper, she showed it to him.

"Some child must have lost this," she said. "Look, the dress is the same kind of flannel we used for Kate's baby."

"It does look like it," John agreed, examining the little figure. "But look, a peg is stuck in the back of its head. That must be there to hang it on the wall."

"I'll ask around next Sunday to see who lost it," Ann decided. "It really is an ugly thing. I can't imagine a child wanting to play with it," she said as she laid it on a shelf by the table.

"Kate still feeling bad?" John asked.

"Her head is really hurting... I took her in some soup, but she hasn't touched it the last time I checked." Going again to Kate's room she saw that she was awake.

"Miss Ann, I Jest don't know what kin be the matter with me," she complained. "My head jest feels like hit be caving in."

"You mean your head aches," Ann corrected her. "Remember, we want to be talking better by the time Tom comes home."

"I guess I jest hurt too bad to remember," Kate went on wearily. "I cain't figure hit out, cause I never get sick. The only other time I ever hurt was when the baby was a'borning."

Ann wondered if Kate had caught something at the party in Gentry. If so, they should know soon. If she did not improve Ann decided she would send for Hattie.

The next day was dismal with snow clouds hanging low over Sawtooth. In the afternoon it began to rain, then sleet. Ann stayed in the cabin and John only went out to get wood and feed the mare. Kate did not improve. Since she had not had any fever, John didn't feel it was necessary to ride the five miles to get Hattie. On the morning of the fourth day after Kate had been in bed, they heard a stomping on the back porch.

"Oh good, company!" Ann exclaimed. Being cooped up in the cabin had began to bore her. She took off her apron and went to the back door with John close behind her. Bud Childers was cleaning his muddy boots on the back steps. His old black hat was dripping and tobacco was oozing out of the corners of his mouth. Still he had a smile for them, even though Ann knew he must be half frozen.

"It sure is good to see you, Mr. Childers," John greeted him. "We've been so lonesome these last few days. What brings you out in this cold weather?"

"Wal, Effie wanted some things from the store, so I jest thought I'd stop off and see would you folks be needing anything. We hain't been off the place fer days. By rights, I should have brung Effie to visit awhile but them clouds shore do look mean to me," Bud continued, looking out through the window.

"You can stay long enough to warm up with some of Ann's hot coffee," John invited.

"Wal, I don't mind if I do," the hill man agreed. Then he started in on his favorite topic. "Ye ort to been with us last week, Preacher," he related. "Me and Bob, and one of them Price boys trailed a fox fer five miles, and them hounds never lost him, in that tracked up snow. They must be lots of timber wolves up under Sawtooth. Looked like they got them a deer by the tracks and blood."

Ann shuddered. "Did you catch the poor fox?" she asked.

"We shore did. Thet there fox won't get in no more hen houses. Why, Effie aims to make her a fur piece out his hide. He was nice and red. Wish I knowed how to fix his head up nice like on them coats in the mail order books." His face was pensive.

"My Aunt Cora has one of those," Ann said. "It always made me nervous when I looked into those beady, glass eyes."

"My Effie ain't a'going to git none like that," Bud replied sadly. "She will have a right smart collar jest the same. That cousin of Yancey's visited here two winters ago and she had a whole coat made of skins. Called hit mink. Must of took nearly fifty pelts to make hit cause she was a right smart big womern."

As Bud got up from the table, he noticed the wooden doll. "Gawd Almighty!" he cried. "Preacher, whar did ye git that thing?" He shrank back from the shelf.

"Ann found it a few days ago out back by the outhouse. We thought some little girl left it last Sunday after service," John said picking up the doll.

"Preacher, put that down and don't ye touch hit agin!" Bud's sharp face was white. "Whar did ye say Kate be?"

"She has a bad headache and has been in bed for four days," Ann replied.

"And whar did thet store-bought pink stuff come from?" Bud asked, pointing at the doll.

"It looks like the flannel we used for Katie's baby, but I don't know how anybody could have gotten a piece of it. Kate has all that was left in her room to put in a quilt," Ann explained.

"Gawd Almighty!" Bud exclaimed again and sank back into his chair. "War there some of thet stuff on the baby when ye buried hit?"

"Yes, there was," Ann replied. "What in the world are you thinking, Mr. Childers?"

"Preacher, we got to pay a visit to thet graveyard right now," Bud commanded. "Come on!"

"Now wait, Bud," John objected, grabbing his arm. "What could this have to do with Kate's baby?"

"Cain't ye see? Somebody thinks Kate is doing bad and they are using witchcraft to get at her. And I bet I know jest who it be! Thet be why Kate is laid up in bed. She won't git no better less ye burn that thang! Throw hit in the fire quick. And I jest bet there hain't no baby in thet grave either. Miss Ann, don't let a soul in here a'fore we git back." He pulled the protesting John out the back door.

Ann stood trembling and irresolute as she heard them leave. What kind of evil was Granny capable of? She remembered the malevolent look and the warning that day on the trail. Quietly she went into Kate's room and found her awake.

"I cain't sleep, Miss Ann. I never knowed how bad a headache could be. Ma used ter have them," she added.

"Kate, I want to ask you about those witch tales. Do you really believe witches can harm you?" she asked, watching Kate's face intently.

"Wal, Pa used ter laugh at them tales, but he must be changed some or he wouldn't hev let old Granny stay there," Kate replied.

"Do you think Granny is a witch?" Ann probed.

"I heered some say so."

"Could she have caused your headache?"

"Shore she could," Kate sat up in her bed and her face blanched. "What be ye trying to tell me?" she asked in alarm.

"Just a minute, Kate. I'll be right back." Ann sped to the kitchen for the doll. "What do you think of this?" she asked holding it out.

"Oh God!" Kate moaned. "Whar did ye get thet?"

"I found it out by the outhouse. Don't be afraid Katie, it's only a doll."

"No hit ain't Miss Ann, no hit ain't! When did ye find hit?" Kate persisted.

"Monday morning," Ann began to be truly frightened.

"I jest knowed hit! That's when I first got bad. Look at thet little peg in the back. And look at thet pink stuff." Katie was shaking as if she had a chill. "Please, Miss Ann, throw that thang in the fire! Maybe I'll git easy if ye do. This be some of old Granny's doings. She thinks I need punishing."

"Do you honestly believe all of this, Kate?" Ann asked, still holding the doll.

"I purely do, Miss Ann. And the quicker ye burn thet thang the better off I be."

"Well, Bud said the same thing, so maybe you are right." Ann walked out to the hearth and threw the crude doll into the fire. To her surprise, flames shot out and seemed almost to touch her. She felt suddenly that all of the stories of evil could be true. If Granny could do this to Kate, what might she do to her and John? She intended to plead with John to go back to Denver. Hurrying back to Kate's room she found her asleep at last.

When Bud and John returned, Ann could tell without even asking that they had bad news.

"The casket was empty," John told her in a low voice. "The dirt was put back just as we left it, but there was snow inside the box, and the pink blanket was gone too."

"I tell ye, Preacher, hit's a witch-master working agin Kate!" Bud lowered his voice, and looked around the room furtively. "Thet thar womern over to Tates' has powers I heerd. Some say she be a witch for sure. Ye would be right smart to send thet girl packing," Bud declared.

"We can't do that. Kate has become very dear to us. Besides, I promised Tom we would take care of her until he gets out of school this spring." John felt he was right. "I believe that God has more power than Satan and he is on our side."

"Thet may be, Preacher," Bud agreed, "but ye had jest better use a little horse sense along with ye depending on God. Hit's a good thang ye burned thet doll. Hit's a pure wonder Kate ain't dead, if hit be thet long since ye found hit."

"She is asleep now, Bud," Ann told him. "It was the strangest thing: one minute she was hurting so bad, and the next she was fast asleep. I just don't understand it."

"Tain't strange a'tall," the little man looked grim. "Ye jest got rid of the hex old Granny was working on her. Now I ain't saying for sure hit be Granny, but hit shore looks that-a-way." Bud's eyes darted nervously around the kitchen.

"At any rate, Bud, let's keep this quiet," John asked. "If it was Granny, she will be wondering why it did not work. Nobody else needs to know that Kate was ill."

"Thet may be all well and good, Preacher," Bud protested, "but ye can jest bet this ain't going to end here. If hit be a body trying to witch Kate, they'll jest try agin. Ye had better take care, believe me! I shore wouldn't want ter be living in the same cabin with the likes of her. Why, they ain't even a horseshoe over the doors! I'll see cain't I find some and bring them over." Bud was twisting his hat in his hands.

"Now, Bud," Ann argued, "you surely don't believe in horseshoes, ladders, and black cats too?"

"I purely do, and ye had better too. If I be ye and the

Preacher, I'd shore git Kate out of here. I'd take her up to Tom's place a'fore the moon comes up."

"No, Bud," John objected. "We won't give in to this evil. We will pray for protection and you'll see that even Granny can't do us any harm."

"Wal, have it yore own way, Preacher, but don't say I never warned ye. I best be gitting on or I'll never git home a'fore dark." Bud looked grim as he went out the door. Looking back he gave a final word. "Ye'll never be able to keep a thing like this here under a barrel, Preacher." He mounted his mule and rode out.

"We must not believe any of this, Ann," John said.

"How can you say that?" Ann objected. "Someone took Kate's baby. Who would do such a terrible thing? When the wooden doll burned up, Katie went straight to sleep. Something very mean is happening here. Who would want a dead baby?" Her voice was strained, and she was in tears. "John, maybe we should leave before something happens to us here."

"I don't deny that there is an evil force working here," John admitted. "I can't explain what happened to Kate's baby, and I don't know why Granny would want it; but please, don't mention this to Katie. We'll wait and tell Tom, then let him tell her."

That evening John prayed for Kate and for all of them that no harm would come. Kate slept through supper, so they did not awaken her. It was a long time before Ann could relax. Every creak of the cabin sounded like someone coming in... even the call of the owls sounded eerie. She knew she deserved to be scared and snuggled closer to John for protection.

A day later a letter arrived from Tom saying he would have a week of vacation for Easter. John decided he would tell him about the baby as soon as he got home. Tom wrote that he had been lucky enough to work for a doctor after school, and was getting useful experience.

Kate was up and feeling much better. She had begun curling

her hair and was trying to look better now. She really was pretty and Ann decided she would help her make a new dress.

The two girls drove with John to Gentry where they lingered over the bolts of gingham, percale, and Indian Head linen.

It was in the general store that Ann heard two local women talking in loud whispers. She knew from their covert looks that they were talking about Kate. Pretending to be interested in buttons, Ann drew Kate to the end of the dim room. But her plan failed, for the voices drew nearer. It seemed the two women intended for Kate to hear what they were saying.

"She shore talks the devil's talk, believe me," Ann heard one of them say. She glanced around the counter and saw the two sunbonnets draw closer together.

"They say thet be why hit war borned dead."

"Shore be a blessing, though, thet the poor little young'un war dead," the other answered. "I heered her Ma is still ailing. I'd shore hate to have Granny after me." Then in a slightly louder voice she added, "if hit war me, thet girl would never stay a night in my cabin!"

Sick at heart, Ann tried pretending that she had not heard the vicious words, but could tell by Katie's stricken face that she had heard. Turning toward the rack of buttons she asked loudly, "Katie, which do you think would look best on that blue print, the white or blue buttons?"

In the silence that followed, Ann heard the women leave. Catching Katie against her, she held her tightly. Damn them, she thought. Why did women have to be so mean to their own kind? Men were not as catty as the women she had known.

"Miss Ann, could Granny Shook cause my baby to be dead?" Kate whispered.

"Of course not!" Ann replied firmly. "Come on, let's go pay Yancey for these things. Tomorrow we'll go over to Hattie's and make your dress." Taking the bolt of blue gingham over to the counter, she noticed Yancey looking curiously at them. As they started to leave he handed Ann a letter. She took the familiar blue envelope and her heart missed a beat. Surely not, she thought… but it was. Bill had finally tracked her down. Slipping the letter into her purse she walked with Kate on out on the porch to wait for John. Soon he came, and they started home.

Ann did not try reading Bill's letter that evening. It lay like a hot coal on her mind. She did tell John what she had heard the women say at the store.

"Those terrible old women said someone caused Kate's baby to die and Kate believes it is Granny!" Ann said. "Can you believe people can be that mean and ignorant?"

"From what I have heard, it seems possible," John admitted. "These people do not know much about the love of God, so they are ruled by fear of anything they can't understand."

"I'd like to give those women a piece of my mind," Ann stated crossly. "Poor Kate felt bad enough as it was." Seeing the look in John's face, she said no more.

After everyone was asleep Ann slipped out and lit the lamp. Slowly she opened the letter. How had Bill traced her? She knew Aunt Cora would never have told him. With dread she read the familiar words of how he loved her, how he missed her, and how he was coming to see her! How would she explain this man to John? God, I need your help now, she thought. Please, please don't let Bill come here. Then she quickly threw the pages into the dying fire.

Early the next morning during breakfast, John reported that the mare was acting up. "I don't know what is wrong. She isn't down, she won't come to her hay, and she won't let me near her. She just stands and rolls her eyes as if she was frightened."

"Did she ever act thet way a'fore?" Kate asked flatly.

"Not since I have had her. Today you would have thought

she'd never seen me before—she won't eat her feed and she tried bolting from the shed."

Kate turned a white face up to John, "Sounds like that mare be witched. I bet old Granny is after us all, and hit be my fault!" She ran and fell into the rocker, sobbing. "I best leave and go away. I best clear out of this holler," she cried.

Ann forgot her own troubles as she tried to comfort the girl. Putting her arms around her, she promised, "We won't let you go anywhere. You are going to stay right here until Tom can take you with him."

"That's right, Kate," John agreed. "We are not afraid of Granny. We know God can defeat her."

"Hit be a comfort to hear ye say so, Preacher," Kate replied through brimming eyes. "But ye jest don't know what can happen in these hills. Jest ye go and ask Hattie. She'll tell ye."

"It looks like we'll have to wait a day or so," John replied, still puzzled about the mare.

"We won't get to go and sew up your new dress, Katie," Ann lamented. "She would pick today to pull her fit." Later on Ann slipped out to the shed to look at the mare. She spoke softly and offered some shelled corn. As the mare rolled her eyes and stamped her feet, Ann shrank back in alarm. John was right. This animal was spooked. Coming back to the kitchen she said nothing, but continued with her cooking.

Kate was remembering stories she had heard as a little girl sitting with her folks around the fire at night. Then, it had been fun to listen to the ghost stories and tales of witches; now, it had become a grim reality. Preacher and Miss Ann didn't know very much and she did not know how to convince them. But she knew Hattie and Jess Wilks might. So Kate held her peace and finished a game of checkers with John just to be polite.

Ann rocked in front of the fireplace. It seemed she could make out Bill's face, laughing at her in the flames. What if he did come and face her here in front of John? That would surely be the end of Mrs. John Nilson. At last she knew she wanted to stay married to John. His love for her suddenly seemed like a warm haven. Oh God, she thought, don't let Bill come here. But in her heart she knew beyond a doubt she was in for a showdown… but how soon?

⊰ Chapter Nine ⊱

Church service the following Sunday was better-attended than usual. Ann noticed two new families with small children. She had looked around nervously, half afraid she might see Bill, but it was soon obvious that Katie was the object of attention. Ann was glad that Hattie and Jess were there, she was anxious to get Hattie alone. Finally, after what seemed like a long time, John turned out his pulpit lamp.

Hattie and Jess walked over to the parsonage and had the fire built up before Ann could get there. When she finally arrived she asked them to stay for lunch and visit before going on home.

"What kin I hep ye do, Mrs. Nilson?" Hattie inquired politely, standing in the door. "We'uns didn't aim to stay, so I hain't got a thing."

"Just sit and talk to me," Ann asked. "Katie and I will soon have dinner on the table. We cooked a nice roast from some of that fresh pork Bud brought us. John bought some sweet potatoes from Yancey's. I have never seen such big, red ones."

"You city folks never git vittles fit to eat," Hattie stated with conviction. "Hit's a pure wonder ter me ye don't all die off. Everything is in a can. The only thing I'd hanker fer be them lights. I shore git tired of cleaning lamps day in and day out."

"Tom says they have electric lights in Siloam Springs," Katie volunteered. "He says we will have them lights too next fall. And they don't be no outhouses," she continued with shining eyes. "They be a room fixed up right inside the house!"

"Hit shore be a caution the way them lights spring on with jest a pull on a string. If I could have one of them, I wouldn't care fer the outhouse being inside. Jess promised to take me to the city some day to see all them things. But the way trapping is this here winter, hit shore won't be anyways soon," Hattie spoke resignedly.

When the food was ready Hattie called into the front room, "You fellers git on in here. These here vittles air gitting cold."

"Yes Ma'am, we air ready," Jess answered with clarity. He sat down beside Ann, putting his old black hat under the chair. "Miss Ann, this here shore looks good to a hungry man." His weathered face was framed by a heavy, red beard. The only time Ann had seen him without his hat on was in church and at her table. She wondered if he slept in it.

"Wal, what do ye think of John's mare?" Hattie asked Jess.

Ann looked up in surprise and saw John's sheepish look. So John had told them.

"Hit's jest like I knowed it war," Jess replied solemnly. "Somebody be witching that there mare. If ye don't do something quick, she won't be fit to ride agin."

"I don't know how to handle an animal that is witched," John said. "This whole business seems so strange and impossible to Ann and me. It doesn't seem it could be possible."

"Wal now," Jess admonished, "ye can see jest how she be acting and taking on. I seen a cow that started giving bloody milk.

It was jest somebody wishing bad luck on the poor feller that owned her."

"How did they cure the cow?" John asked with interest.

"Wal now," Jess said sheepishly, "they sent fer one of them power doctors and he boiled some of the milk, near as I recollect. Seems hit shore worked, cause the cow got over hit."

"My pappy used to have a remedy fer witched cattle," Hattie said. "There be a womern lived jest over the line from us in Missouri. She caused trouble with folks around there. Pa said she be a young womern too. They cooked up some burnt corn-pone and put soot in hit. When they fed hit to the stock along with their hay, they usually got over any spooking. I remember hearing tell some fed hit to their young'uns too."

"That must taste awful," Ann shuddered.

"That is the most incredible thing I ever heard," John said. "I just can't believe that such a thing can work."

"John, it could happen," Ann told him seriously. "I have seen a lot of mean people. Maybe there is someone that mean here. You said yourself Satan has more power in the world than God!"

"Could be," John replied, "but I don't see how our feeding burnt cornbread to the poor mare would do any good."

"Wal, ye can snicker if ye want, and jest keep on walking," Jess stated. "If ye ask me, this here ain't no time to be jest setting still."

"John," Ann asked, "why not go ahead and try it? You might as well try."

"If spooking yore mare is all thet old she-cat does to ye, I'd say ye be right lucky," Jess advised. "But I bet ye as long as Kate be here, they be meanness a'foot."

"Thet be what I told them," Kate agreed sadly, "but the preacher says he aims fer me to stay. I jest hate to think I be the cause of their bad luck."

"Wal, if hit gits too fierce, I know a body who jest might give old Granny a few fits too," Jess promised. "Mind ye, I don't hold none with this here witching, but I heered tell hit works. We don't want hit to git started agin around our holler."

"Nothing like that will happen, Jess. We are not afraid of Granny. We know God will protect us. Satan still trembles when God speaks."

"Jest the same, ye get Kate to cook up a pan of soot and corn-meal fer thet mare," Jess ordered. "It be no use ye being stubborn. Ye need her to ride. If the first batch don't do hit, fetch her some more. Ye'll see hit will shore do the job."

"All right, Jess," John gave in. "I guess it won't hurt, but my convictions are against it."

"Now be sure and let us know if anything else goes wrong, Preacher," Hattie said. "We don't aim to set by and let anything bad happen to you folks. We need fer ye to stay."

"That is kind of you, Hattie," John replied gratefully.

After the Wilks' left, Kate mixed the cornbread under Ann's and John's incredulous eyes. After beating up what would have been a nice pan of bread, Kate dumped in a cup of old black soot that she had scraped from the inside of the fireplace. Ann wondered what Aunt Cora would say if she knew about this.

She joined John before the fire and they sat in thoughtful silence. They heard Kate go out of the back door to take the awful mess to the mare. By tomorrow they would know if Hattie's remedy worked.

During the night Ann heard rain lashing the cabin, and the tree limbs creaking and rubbing against the roof. Sleeping fitfully, she thought morning would never come. The day crept in so dismal, and sharp winds and sleet continued until almost noon. The pines were dripping and the wind sent small showers against the windows. She wondered what the animals did when they could not get out to hunt for food.

Soon John put on his heavy coat, took an apple, and went to

the shed. Ann and Kate watched patiently at the window until he returned.

"How is she?" Ann asked anxiously.

"Did she eat the cornpone?" Katie wanted to know.

"Yes, she did, and some of her hay. And she let me brush her. I'd say that our little mare is over her mad spell." John's face reflected his amazement.

"Didn't she wall her eyes at ye, Preacher?" Katie persisted.

"No, she was quite calm," John replied. "Now, I know you think it was that mess you fixed up and fed her, but it could just as well have been she got over whatever had ailed her."

"Ye kin believe what ye want, but I know jest as well as I be Kate Matthews, thet mare was witched," Kate said.

So the matter rested. The mare got over her fright and John was able to ride to the store again to stock up on things they needed. He also brought home some mail and some news— Katie's mother was worse. Ann thought she had never seen anything as interesting as the Sears catalog. Later, she helped Kate cut out her new dress.

The next day was spent at Hattie's, sewing up the long seams on her treadle machine. Since nothing else had happened to alarm them, the subJect of witches was avoided by Ann.

In the last week of March the air seemed to change. Ann felt it early one morning and commented on it at breakfast.

"Ye be a smart one," Kate told her. "It shore feels like spring is coming. If hit is, ye will see some powerful water running. One year old Bitter Creek took part of Price's sheds and logs right down to Gentry."

"We surely won't have that much water around here," John speculated. "It's half a mile to Burnt Creek. But Tom's place is real close. Perhaps I ought to check on Tom's mother when it does rise."

"Hit shore wouldn't hurt none," Kate agreed. "Thet husband

of her's built too close to the creek. He was a city feller you know. Smart in books but dumb ever place else. They say he left a whole lot of them books too."

"Yes, I saw them last fall," John agreed. "They gave Tom his incentive to read. But most of them are about engineering, and Tom doesn't seem interested in that."

"Being a doctor will be better," Ann said in defense of Tom.

"I wish I could read them all," Kate sighed, as her thoughts flew to Tom. Spring vacation seemed so far away.

Suddenly Ann remembered Bill's letter. In the turmoil over the mare she had forgotten it. She wouldn't answer it and hoped he would let her alone. Still she knew Bill never let "his possession" go without a fight.

⚘ Chapter Ten ⚘

They awoke one morning to find the hollow warm and sparkling with sunshine. John announced he would ride up and see about Mrs. Matthews. He saddled up the mare and started up the trail that ran along the creek. To his amazement, Burnt Creek was a torrent of muddy water. Limbs and small trees were being tumbled along by the swift current. Alarmed, he quickened the mare's pace.

In the boiling flood he saw a chicken coop sailing swiftly amid torn out bushes and trees. In some places the creek looked fifty feet across. He worried about the old bridge at Gentry, where two creeks spilled into the river that flowed toward Siloam Springs. As far as he knew the bridge had never been torn away. When he came into sight of Tom's home, he sighed in relief. A thin ribbon of smoke rose from the chimney. He knew Mrs. Matthews was there and had made a fire. Looking down toward the creek, he saw that her outhouse and barn were under water.

Riding on in, he tied the mare up and knocked on the door. Almost instantly the bar slid back and a worried face looked out at him. John was shocked by her appearance. Her hair tangled around her face, not in its usual neat bun. Her dress was muddy and she was barefoot.

"What happened to you?" he asked. "Surely you haven't been out in all that water!"

"Had to let old Maudie out," the old woman whined. "We jest cain't git by less we keep thet mule. I jest turned her in the cornfield. Nothing much left to worry about. Cain't find the old sow. Had one pig left to fatten. Wish I had a son thet would stay home and take care of his ma!" She moved to the fire, and spread her skirt to the flames to dry.

"I was concerned and decided to ride up and see how you were. We heard from Tom last week, that is Katie did. He will be home a short while at Easter. Do you think the water could rise up to the house?"

"Never has since I been here, and thet be a good long time," she answered. "If that creek gits much higher though, it shore could take the barn." She pulled on her high-top shoes, and started to pin up her hair.

"We would be happy to have you come and stay with us until this danger is over," John offered. "You could help the girls with their sewing."

"Ain't going ter stay near thet Kate. Tad Price done told me all about her last week when he brought me some meal. Says the whole county be talking about how her poor ma is laying in bed, cause she been sinning. More's the pity my poor Tom done a fool thing as to take up with the likes of her." Mrs. Matthews' face was red with anger.

"Surely you can't blame Kate for her mother's being sick?" John asked in surprise.

"From what I heerd, Granny Shook thinks she be to blame."

"And I suppose you think she is absolutely right?" John

asked indignantly. "It could be that she has arthritis like several others around this area."

"Hit be shore funny she never had hit until after Kate broke out and got herself a young'un, now ain't hit? Wal, let it be yore way. I jest ain't going to yore cabin and she ain't coming to live in mine. Tom kin jest face thet when he gits back. If'n he don't care fer his ma enough to stay here and work this farm, he jest don't need to come home a'tall."

"I'm sorry to hear you say that because he wrote that he wants to do up your work while he's here. He'll be disappointed."

"Wal, he kin come home if he be a mind to, but he cain't no way bring that Kate onto this here place, and I mean hit."

"Is there anything I can do for you while I am here?" John asked resignedly. He now knew it was useless to argue about Tom and Kate.

"I'd shore like to get that corn moved up behind the house. I tried to use the cart, but thet water is jest too high fer me. I could give ye Tom's big boots," she said in a softer tone.

"Fine," John agreed, relieved at her quick reversal in attitude. Where there was a need, there was usually a way he knew. Mrs. Matthews needed her son on any terms and John felt sure that Kate would finally be accepted too. Sloshing back and forth from the barn, he saw the water was slowly rising and wondered if it would reach the house. The cabin was built on a little rise and John doubted if the creek could rise that high. After moving the grain, he came back to the fire to dry out. The hill woman was a bit more civil and gave him a cup of hot coffee. While he was busy drinking it she yielded to her curiosity.

"Hain't ye and yer missus a'feared of what old Granny might do to ye?" she asked.

"No, we are not afraid of Granny, or anyone else who might be doing devilish things," John replied. "I am a witness for God here, and I don't believe he'll let Granny harm either Kate or us."

John was glad she had asked the question because it gave him an opening to express his views to the hill woman. She probably had never heard the gospel.

Promising to come back soon, John rode off in a rising wind that eventually gave way to sleet, driving into his face as he rode. Pulling his coat collar closer, he felt sorry the mare had to face the onslaught with a burden on her back. Well, he had a burden too. Sometimes when he looked at Ann he could almost guess her thoughts. She had to be comparing this life to the old days of living in luxury in Denver. He felt he had been a fool to think he could make a girl like Ann happy. Also he knew she did not know his God like he did. At the time, he had felt she would change and that his love would be enough. They had been here almost a year now and he still saw wistful looks and frowns when things went wrong. That man Bill must have been special. Well, all he could do was pray for his own miracle. It could happen, he knew.

It was a solid hour before he came within sight of the parsonage. John knew they were waiting for him with a good, hot supper; but he also knew he must care for the mare first. As he rubbed her down and forked down some hay, a sudden gust shook the shed and sleet pelted the tin roof. It was barely sundown and was now quite dark. Bending low, he raced for the shelter of the back porch. As he scraped off his boots, he smelled the tantalizing odor of fresh baked bread and noticed the warmth of the lamp as it shone through the window. How we treasure the light, he thought.

"Hit's about time ye got here," Kate greeted him. "We been a mite worried. How be Tom's ma?"

"Girls, you'd never believe how wide Burnt Creek is," he began. "Why, you could float a wagon right on that stream! Ann, when I go back I'd like you to go too. Maybe you can persuade Tom's mother to come and stay with us until the danger is over.

It could take her barn, and might even get up to the house. You know, I forgot about her wood. I hope it doesn't float away."

"Why wouldn't she come with you today?" Ann asked.

John hesitated and tried not to look at Kate. "She was so sure it wouldn't reach the house that she didn't want to leave."

"She won't come as long as I be here," Kate stated flatly.

"Now Katie, I'm sure that wasn't the reason. She was just afraid of the water," Ann told her, yet knowing all the time Kate was right.

"We won't worry about it tonight," John said.

"Maybe by tomorrow the creek will recede. Now let me have some of that bread I could smell half the way home!" So the subject was forgotten in the comfort of warm food and a good fire.

The next day was calm and clear with a warm sun shining. John could still hear the roar of the creek, but upon investigation found that it had lost some of its thunder. Surely the Matthews' place will be all right, he reasoned. But Ann did not feel that easy.

"I think you should go back. You'd never forgive yourself if anything did happen up there. I really don't want to go, and besides, you can ride so much faster alone," she said.

So, after attending to the stoves and bringing plenty of wood to the back porch, John left.

Ann decided to walk down and look at the creek. She tried as best as she could to put her fear of Granny out of her mind. Katie had not wanted to go and Ann was glad to have a chance to be alone. The air smelled so fresh and everything looked clean and new. She thought of all the flowers waiting to break through the moist ground. Hemlock needles softly crunched under her feet as she walked under the forest canopy and the branches rustled over her head from the wind. She saw clouds tumbling across the cracks in the canopy above, and she knew this warmth would not last.

As she walked, the roar of Burnt Creek grew until it finally drowned out all other sounds. Rounding a curve in the trail, she saw the muddy, rolling water carry a large timber, which must have come from the mill, upstream. Nature could be vicious, she thought and moved back from the ugly water. After a few minutes of watching the rushing torrent, she started back down the trail towards home. The sun had disappeared and the light had faded. A sudden chill came over her and she wished she had not disobeyed John. I am always doing some fool, stupid thing, she chided herself. It was then that she saw the enormous yellow cat. Its slanted, amber eyes seemed to glow like live coals as they stared right through her. She knew in that instant how scared a mouse must feel.

Chiding herself, she wondered who it belonged to and called out to the cat. Her overture was not accepted. The cat arched its back, spit fiercely, then turned and ran away through the trees. Ann urgently quickened her pace toward home. When she reached the clearing, she was surprised to see the Wilks' wagon tied behind the parsonage. Inside she found Hattie, Kate, and Jess talking at the kitchen table.

"Oh Hattie, it's good to see you and Jess," she exclaimed with pleasure. "What are you doing way down here?"

"Wall," Hattie hesitated, "we'uns jest been telling Kate here that we been feeling uneasy about ye and the preacher. So we been bound to come see if hit war alright with ye and Kate."

"I guess John won't be back for awhile from Mrs. Matthews' place," Ann told them. "The creek is really high and he was worried about her. I guess Katie told you he was up there yesterday."

"Kate's been telling me about thet old womern," Hattie snorted. "Guess her feathers air still ruffled about her only young'un getting married."

"Oh, I'm sure she will come around in time," Ann hastened to reply, noticing Kate's troubled face. To change the subject she asked, "Who around here owns a big, yellow cat? I met the largest one I have ever seen a few minutes ago on my way back from the creek."

"Yaller cat?" Jess asked, sitting up straight. "Whar at did ye see hit?"

"Quite a way back toward the creek. About halfway I think. It certainly wasn't very friendly. It spat at me in the fiercest way. Do you think someone moved away, left it, and it went wild?" This seemed logical to Ann.

"That warn't no earthly cat, Mrs. Nilson," Hattie spoke soberly. "The next time hit shows up, ye jest holler 'Witch, Witch' at the top of your lungs. That there cat will make tracks, ye can jest bet on hit. And hit won't bother ye no more."

"You mean that the cat belongs to a witch?" Ann asked.

"Thet cat war the witch," Jess stated grimly. "I heered tell of a yaller cat once over to Missouri, and ever time when hit showed up, somebody up and died."

"I hope hit ain't going to happen here," Kate worried.

Ann poured a cup of coffee with shaking hands and sat down at the table. She was frightened and wished that John would return. With a firmness she did not feel, she answered Jess.

"Wherever the cat came from, Jess, it isn't likely that I'll ever see it again. Besides, whoever heard of a cat doing anything bad?"

"Ye kin laugh at hit all ye please," Jess stated, "but jest remember what Hattie says, 'cause old Granny is shore got the evil eye on ye all here."

It was with genuine relief later when Ann heard John ride in and tie up at the back porch. Getting up quickly she went to open the door for him. Amid the general greetings, John told them that Mrs. Matthews was fine and that the creek had not risen higher.

"It had me worried yesterday," John told them. "I was surprised to see how wide and swift that little creek had become. I am afraid all of the good fishing holes Tom and I tried will be washed away."

"Don't ye fret none about thet," Jess reassured him. "Them smart fellers all come home. They get back somehow."

"I am glad to hear that," John smiled. "A smart grandaddy catfish got the best of me all last fall. I hope to get another try at him when Tom comes home."

Catching up on the news of the hollows, drinking coffee, and sampling the stewed apple pie Hattie had made, kept them all away from the subject of witches. Ann was glad not to have to face the subject again. As the Wilks drove away, she knew she would have to talk to John about the cat. In a way she was grateful when Katie brought the subject up.

"Preacher, did ye see airy strange critter when ye war riding back from Mother Matthews'?" she asked.

"What kind do you have in mind?" John queried. "I saw plenty of wild things today... I guess they all know that spring is coming. There were squirrels poking around and I saw buzzards circling up on Sawtooth. On the way back the wind came up so there was not much life visible."

"I kind of had a yaller cat in mind," Kate persisted, watching him intently.

"That is odd," John began, with a puzzled look. "I did see a big, yellow cat a couple of nights ago when I went out to feed the mare. I meant to ask you whose it was, but it seemed too wild to be a pet. When I called, it spit at me, and took off through the brush. What made you ask about a yellow cat?"

"Hattie and Jess seem to think that cat is a witch. Something of Granny Shook's doings," Ann explained lamely. "You see, I saw it too this afternoon when I walked down to look at the creek. The cat was so big and fierce looking." Ann felt uncomfortable under John's accusing gaze. "I am sorry, John, but I just wanted to see the creek after what you said about it being so wide."

"Dear, surely you are not putting credence in these tales of witchcraft. All of that talk is just superstition. You and Katie forget it—nothing is going to happen to us here. Now quit this worrying." After stating his position, John went out to put away and feed the mare.

During the night, Ann heard the wind get stronger and howl around the cabin. Dead vines rustled outside her window. She wished she had as much faith in God as John did. She also wished she had made a clean breast of her past before she had married John. God, she thought, let me be happy here. At last she felt she had found a purpose to her life in loving this good man and being a helper to him.

~ Chapter Eleven ~

The blustery weather continued, but the thaw persisted and Burnt Creek finally settled down to its normal gurgle. Ann and Katie had been trying to decide where to put their vegetable garden, and finally decided upon the plot that was used by the last preacher there.

"The preacher they had here didn't plant hardly a thing," Kate informed them. "Pa said he be the laziest man that ever set foot in this here holler."

"How did your father know if he didn't go to the services?" Ann asked.

"Wal," Kate elaborated, "hit war common talk to Gentry. They said all he had were taters, squashes and onions. They don't take no care. Then he war too lazy to dig them taters, so they jest rotted right in the ground. This patch had orta be rich. Jess came over once to hep him and they ended up going fishing. He knowed thet folks would feed him and his young'uns, so he jest didn't care. Ye and the preacher had best git word to Jess to bring his mule over and git this patch plowed. If them taters and onions and such hain't planted in the next few days, the moon will be fulling agin."

"I've heard of planting in the full of the moon," Ann observed, "but I never did understand why."

"Wal, you best put in onions, beets, turnips, carrots, and them things thet grows down under, while it be the dark of the moon. Then ye kin put out the beans, peas, tomaters, squashes, and such in two or three weeks. But git word to Jess first to git over here and plow up this here patch. We kin git seeds at Yancey's store. If I could see Ma, she'd give us some, but I know Pa would never do hit. Hattie may send ye some though."

Ann was surprised at the interest John showed in their garden; when he offered to take them to the store for supplies, they decided to make a holiday of it. Kate packed a lunch and they planned to eat it at some nice place along the creek. Fluffy clouds were moving across the sky, but spring was in the air. The late March sun felt warm and the earth was beginning to dry out. The blue mist rising in the valley seemed more like smoke: it swirled and eddied as they drove through the forest. When they came to a sunlit clearing it seemed like they were entering a golden light. Ann caught a glimpse or two of bright eyes watching, and laughed aloud. John looked down, caught her smile, and his heart lifted. Maybe spring would change her mind about his place of service here.

At Yancey's store several men were swapping stories and chewing tobacco. Yancey was a big man with a ruddy face. Very little hair was left on his head, and what was left had turned dirty orange, suggesting that it was once red. Yancey had learned to listen and not talk too much during his years in the store. John had been quick to learn from his example. Yancey had operated the store almost thirty years, but was still referred to as that city feller by the older people. His wife was small and seemed meek, but John soon learned she could spread gossip into each holler and every cabin. This day Rose Yancey was sitting in a rocker on the porch of their rooms that adjoined the store.

"Sure is a fine day," Ann called to her. "What are you working on there, Mrs. Yancey?"

"It's some blocks for the quilting bee next week. This is the flower garden pattern. I always like to make this one because of the pretty colors. They are going to quilt a cover for the Tatum girl who lives up close to Price's. She's getting married soon." Rose held up the hexagon shaped pieces for Ann to admire. It was amazing how the tiny pieces formed a flower, set off by little green pieces used to make leaves. They were not much larger than a dollar.

"I know about Mary Tatum," Katie remarked. "She be going to marry some feller from Little Rock. He was up to the mill last spring selling new saws or some such like, and he saw Mary, they say."

"Kate, why don't you and Mrs. Nilson come to the quilting too? It's to be at Hattie's. I'm sure she meant to ask you. Everyone always has such a good time, and we have good things to eat. Everyone brings a dish you know," Rose looked expectantly at Ann.

"Maybe we will," Ann agreed. "That is if John can take us. It will be good to visit everyone we haven't seen for a long time."

"Shore will," Kate said, "and we can catch up on all the news. Maybe they been to see Ma."

Ann hurried Katie into the store before Rose could get started. She didn't want Kate upset again about her mother and she suspected Rose was bursting to tell some new gossip tidbit. Inside the floor creaked; and the pungent smells of kerosene, tobacco, leather, and cheese filled the air. Yancey came over to offer assistance.

"Mr. Yancey," Ann began, looking up at him, "we need some

seeds to start a spring garden. Give us the easiest things to grow, because this is my first time to ever grow anything."

"Why sure, Miss Ann," Yancey smiled. "I bet Katie here can give you a hand. Her pa has one of the best gardens around every year. Let's see, you'll want carrots, beans, beets, some squash, and peas. Were you going to put in potatoes too?"

"Wal no," Kate interrupted. "Jess Wilks will bring us all the taters we need. He always does fer the preachers."

Ann could see the hill men had noted their conversation and were mentally betting on how far her garden would get. Well, she would show them, she vowed.

"Oh yes, Mr. Yancey, I'll also need some gardening gloves, a hoe, a rake, and what else would you say, Katie?

"Thet will do fer a starter, Miss Ann," Katie answered sheepishly, "unless we wants to git some licrish drops too!" Turning around, she saw the amused glances being exchanged by the circle of onlookers. "We best git," she told Ann in a low voice. "Air there a letter fer me, Mr. Yancey?" she asked. Yancey went inside the little cage and looked.

"Nothing today, Kate. I guess your young man is busy now getting ready for spring exams."

"Thet shore be right. Tom has a lot of books he be studying," Kate stated with pride and gave the hill men a satisfied look.

They took the sacks of seeds and candy and Yancey followed them out to the springboard with the tools. They had left John a mile back as he had wanted to look in on one of the hill men who was laid up with a fever.

"Mr. Yancey, if ye see Jess Wilks a'fore Sunday, tell him the preacher needs him to plow up thet strip behind the parsonage," Katie said.

"Sure and I will, Miss Kate," the big man promised, as he helped Kate and Ann into the wagon and untied the mare. "You had best tell the preacher to be careful about taking sides with the Holcombs. I know he's good-hearted; but that feud has been going on ever since I've been here and he is not going to be able to settle it." Yancey's blue eyes were serious.

In alarm Ann turned to Kate. "What does he mean, Kate?"

"Oh, reckon he be jest a'talking on that fuss thet they been having as long as I been born. Old Man Holcomb run off with one of the Jones girls over in Missouri and brung her here to live. The Joneses follered them as far as the top of Sawtooth. They been shooting at each other off and on fer a long time. Thet's why Leon Holcomb is in bed and the preacher be there." Kate had tried to make light of the story.

"It isn't quite that simple, Miss Ann," Yancey insisted. "I am sure John will be trying to get them to make up, so thought I should tell you."

First witchcraft and now feuds and shootings! Why was she here in this hillbilly jungle? she wondered. Swaying in the spring seat as Kate held the reins on the mare, Ann's thoughts ran wild. She had read about feuds and killings, but had not believed it. Kate's voice broke her thoughts.

"They been three Holcombs kilt and two Joneses that I heerd of, and maybe more way back," Katie elaborated. "Guess Yancey knows more about hit though."

"John will try I know," Ann worried. "I know him and he always tries to make peace."

"Thet be real bad," Katie answered. "Family fights be strictly hands-off in these here hills. Them that try shore be asking fer trouble."

When the mare pulled up in front of the Holcomb cabin, Ann looked with interest at the weather-beaten structure. It was built in two sections, high up off the ground, with a porch all of the way around and a breezeway joining the two sections. Ann guessed that one section contained the kitchen, and the other the sleeping rooms. The place looked even more neglected than others she had seen: weeds choked the path that led to the rickety porch; a little barefoot girl peeked around the corner of the cabin; an immense three-legged iron pot, which Ann knew must be the washing pot, sat in a pile of ashes; chickens pecked around the scattered pieces of firewood; and a baying hound raced out to announce their presence. Kate did not have time to tie up the mare before John was out on the porch.

"Girls, come in for a minute and meet the Holcombs," he invited, helping them down.

Ann was not anxious to go inside, but knew she should being the preacher's wife. Slowly she followed Katie into the big front room. There were several beds piled up with quilts and feather pillows. On one bed was propped an unshaven, red-headed man. Against the wall was a long plank table with several tow-headed children sitting behind it on a bench.

"Ann and Kate, meet Lonny Holcomb and his wife Sally," John directed.

Sally held her hand out shyly. She was pretty, with an innocent, natural manner. Her blonde hair was combed neatly, but she too was barefoot. She looked curiously at Ann, noting her dress, and especially her wedding ring. Her husband, Lonny, made no comment but was staring at Kate. Ann could see that this room seemed to be a living, eating, and also a sleeping room. A ladder led up to the loft where there were husks of spotted corn and tobacco hanging from the rafters.

"Come warm yerself by the fire," Sally invited. Ann walked over and held her cold hands to the blaze. One of the tow-heads sidled over to Katie.

"Whatcher buy ter the store?" the little boy asked eagerly. Katie turned to Ann with a look of surprise.

"We got seeds ter make a garden," Kate answered.

"We also got a bag of licorice drops, Katie," Ann chided. "Why don't you go out and get them?"

"You young'uns set down and shet up," Lonnie commanded from his bed. The tow-headed boy immediately dodged behind the table, but grinned broadly when Kate went out of the door.

"Mr. Holcomb has been quite ill," John hastened to explain to Ann. "We've been talking and he has promised to bring the children to services as soon as he is up and around."

Ann distinctly heard a snicker from behind the table. She wondered if they had decent clothes to go anywhere. It was too cold yet to be barefoot and she realized that they probably did not own any shoes.

"Do youn'ses tell stories and play games?" one boy asked.

"Well, no," John answered. "But we do read about Jesus and the things he used to do, even when he was young like you."

"Sometimes we have a treat for the young folks," Ann added.

"All they do is think on eating," Lonnie complained. "Since that dirty Tad Jones got me, I hain't been able ter hunt none a'tall. Most of our vittles air gone. Guess I'll jest hev to send word to old Uncle Bep t'other side of Gentry. I hep him with planting and he heps we'uns out come lean times." The hill man closed his eyes in resignation. Ann could see the customary black hat hanging on a peg over his bed.

"I've heard of your Uncle Bep," John said with interest. "Didn't he preach around here at one time?"

"Yup, shore did. They was a'fore they built thet meeting house whar ye air now. Uncle Bep didn't hanker to go so fur jest to tell how bad we all be. So when they sent a city preacher, he jest stayed with his farming. But ain't none ever been here thet can hold a candle to him. He knows airy word in the good book, he do." Lonnie's voice held a note of pride.

"I'd like to meet him sometime," John answered with sincerity. "I'm sure he would be very interesting to talk to." Turning to Katie as she came back in he added, "Give Lonnie some of those drops for his cough. This shoulder will heal faster if he doesn't cough so much." As he turned to leave, Lonnie took hold of his hand.

"Preacher, we been hearing a lot of talk about the trouble up to yore place. You think I been having it, but ye shore ort to be careful. That old womern is sure after ye, and I bet it's on account of Kate." He looked curiously at the girls as they went out on the porch.

"Don't worry about her, Lonny. God is on our side, and she can't harm us." John spoke more bravely than he felt. "Kate has become very dear to us. She'll stay with us until Tom can take care of her."

Out on the porch Ann saw the wistful look on Sally's pale face. "Why don't you come to the quilting party at Hattie's? It would do you good to get out."

"Hit sure would pleasure me," Sally beamed, "thet is, if Lonn will let me."

"Miss Ann means well," Katie whispered. "Ye come if ye can."

The ride home was made with little conversation: Katie was thinking about what she had overheard Lonny saying to John; John was sick at heart because of the ignorance of these people; Ann was angry at the injustices of life to the poor, little woman she had just seen. Half of the men in this world needed to be horse-whipped, Ann thought. It was the women and the kids who suffered. Well, she wasn't going to be treated that way ever. And as for having kids... she didn't think so.

⊰ Chapter Twelve ⊱

On the day of the quilting bee Katie was very excited. "I wonder what pattern they will make up for Mary?" she asked Ann. "They be so many purty ones. There be the Dutch Doll, Wishbone, Bow Tie, Wedding Ring, and always the plain old string quilt."

"Remember, Rose said it was going to be the flower garden one," Ann answered.

Katie was carefully tucking a white cloth around the basket of cookies that she had helped Ann make. Ann had decided to take a can of store-bought coffee. Most of the hill women ground their own beans and they loved the finer grind from the store. Soon John had the wagon ready for them. He was planning on dropping them off then continuing on up the mountain to visit some of the families there.

When they arrived at the Wilks, Ann and Katie stepped into Hattie's crowded front room where several women were already bent over the quilting frames.

"Hit shore pleasures me, Mrs. Nilson, thet ye got to come," Hattie exclaimed, her blue eyes shining. "I'm glad the word got to ye. This here be Mary Tatum," she explained, turning to a slight, pale girl who didn't look over fifteen, "and this here is her Aunt Sairy." She pointed to an old woman in a faded gingham dress. "Folks, here be Mrs. Nilson, the preacher's wife, and ye all know Kate."

"I'm so glad to meet all of you," Ann said, looking over the curious faces and knowing she was on inspection.

"Now while you'nses are quilting, maybe Mrs. Nilson can read to us. I bet she never done no quilting a'fore," Hattie laughed along with the others.

"You are right about that," Ann admitted. "What do you want me to read?" She hoped they didn't intend for her to teach the Bible. If they knew how little she knew, they would be surprised. Hattie brought her Bible and pointed to Psalm 121. So Ann read:

> [1]I will lift up mine eyes unto the hills, from whence cometh my help.
> [2]My help cometh from the Lord, which made heaven and earth.
> [3]He will not suffer thy foot to be moved: he that keepeth thee will not slumber.
> [4]Behold, he that keepeth Israel shall neither slumber nor sleep.
> [5]The Lord is thy keeper: the Lord is thy shade upon thy right hand.
> [6]The sun shall not smite thee by day, nor the moon by night.
> [7]The Lord shall preserve thee from all evil: he shall preserve thy soul.
> [8]The Lord shall preserve thy going out and thy coming in from this time forth, and even for evermore.

"Oh my, hain't thet purty," Hattie sighed.

"Wal, hit seems we'uns have a heap of evil in these hills," Grandma Tatum observed with relish as her needle flashed in and out of the quilt. Ann wondered if she was referring to the Holcombs and Jones feud, or to the trouble with Granny Shook. Effie Childers soon enlightened her.

"I heerd tell old man Jones shore got that Holcomb feller. Caught him on the trail up to the mill."

"And they say Granny be staying up thar at the Jones' fer a spell," Granny Tatum added with a sly look at Kate.

"Wal, at least Lucy will git a rest if'n she be gone," Hattie replied with a vengeance. "Katie, did ye know yer ma was up and setting on the porch last week? Jess seen her when he went by one day."

"I'd shore like to see Ma," Kate sighed. "Wish I could jest ketch Pa gone to town sometime. I shore be glad thet Ma is doing better."

"Katie, we'll drive over there next week to see your mother," Ann promised. "I'm sure your father can't do us any harm. If Granny Shook has gone, he may be a lot calmer. Isn't it wonderful that your mother is better now? I have heard that the warm sun does a lot of good for people with arthritis." Looking around for a safe subject to discuss, she noticed a beautiful collar on one woman's dress. "That certainly is beautiful crochet you have on your dress," she remarked to the startled hill woman.

"Tain't crochet," the old woman answered amid the titters of the group. "This hyar is tatting. So is thet doily under them pictures of Hattie's."

"I guess I'm pretty ignorant," Ann smiled. "I haven't seen anything so dainty anywhere. What is tatting?"

"Wal, ye use a shuttle," Hattie explained, getting out her handmade, bone shuttle to show Ann. "This'n here was made by my pappy fer my ma. When her eyes give out she give hit to me. Some day I'll give hit to Lettie May fer her to use."

"I am impressed with all of the beautiful things you ladies make," Ann said with honesty. "Lovely quilts, crochet, knitting, and now this beautiful tatting. You can all of your vegetables, and jams and jellies, then make most of your clothes too."

"There be weaving too, Miss Ann," Katie added. "My ma made the purtiest things fer me... she'd color the cloth with roots and barks. But them days is shore over. Poor Ma cain't hardly do her churning and baking these days."

"How did she make colors?" Ann asked curiously.

"Wal," Hattie explained, "there be pokeberries fer the lavender, hickory bark fer yaller, madder fer red, walnut hulls fer brown and black, and indigo fer blue. There be more but I cain't recollect them."

"I'll never get over being surprised by the skills you ladies have," Ann praised them, realizing that she meant it. They weren't so dumb after all. But why did they let men treat them so badly?

Soon Hattie spread out the food on her long, plank table in the kitchen. Ann could hardly believe it. There was fried chicken, pies, turnovers, and egg salad just to start. And everyone seemed to enjoy Ann's coffee. She realized with surprise that she was actually enjoying this backwoods gathering. All too soon John came back from the mountain and it was time to go.

"Thank you for a lovely time," Ann turned to Hattie. "Katie and I have enjoyed being here."

"We'uns shore be glad to see ye too," Hattie beamed. "Air ye going over to the Tates?"

"We shore will if'n the preacher will take us," Kate vowed. "I aim to see my Ma fer sure. Pa ain't so bad when thet Granny ain't around."

"Wal, jest be wary of her. Jest cause they say she is up to Sawtooth don't mean she cain't appear in a minute. They say she comes right sudden jest when a body ain't looking fer her. I'd purt near rather be in hell with my back broke than have thet old womern after me." Several of the hill women nodded their heads in solemn agreement.

Ann was frightened by the vehemence in Hattie's voice and turned to the door. She hurried Kate out to the wagon before anything else could be said. They drove off after a chorus of good-byes from those on the porch.

"It sounds like you girls were a hit," John observed in relief.

"Mostly curiosity," Ann explained. "Oh, I really didn't mean that, John," she apologized, seeing the disappointed look on his face. "They really were nice to us, and the food was very good. The only thing is they would rather talk about Granny and feuding than nicer things."

"Now you know how women are, just the same as in Denver," John teased. "They always have to talk about someone." He knew they were curious about Ann. He also knew they thought she was ignorant and would starve if it wasn't for him.

"Anyways, we heerd that old Granny has gone up to Sawtooth, and so Miss Ann says we can go see Ma. We heered she's up now."

"That is right," Ann agreed. "When do you think you can take us over there?"

"I promised Holcomb I'd come and help him tomorrow," John answered regretfully. "They want my help in writing up an order for some apple trees."

"The only thing Lonny Holcomb ever raised was kids and sweet taters," Kate voiced in disbelief.

"I know," John answered patiently, "but I've been trying to get some of these farmers here to put in apple trees. The ones they have now are mostly scrubs. Up around Siloam Springs they have fine orchards. There's no reason apples wouldn't do well here. And with one evaporator for the whole area, they could have a good money crop that would provide work for the young people. Anyway, how about if I take you girls over to Tates' place the next day?"

"That will work out fine," Ann agreed. "Then we'll have a day to bake some bread and goodies for Lucy."

As she smelled the sweet aroma of the bread the next day, Ann realized she was anticipating seeing Kate's mother. She hoped Eli would not act so mean. If he did, she intended to tell him how mean he was. Thinking about it made her mad. Every time things settled down to enjoyment, she thought about how shaky her security was. Her thoughts were interrupted by Kate.

"I wish we had something to take Pa," she remarked plaintively. "He never used much tobacco, nor spirits. But Bud told Ma he seen Pa hide a bottle in the barn one time. I never put much stock in it though."

"We'll think of something," Ann promised. "I want you and your mother to enjoy your visit."

Driving through the woods the next morning was a sweet, delightful treat for Ann. As they crossed a small stream, she saw trout playing tag in the clear water.

"John, how can you stand to hook them?" she asked.

"Now, you know I throw the little ones back," John smiled. "Besides, they were made for man to eat."

"Oh, I'd like to have some of that watercress to take to Lucy," Ann requested, pointing. "Can we stop here for a minute?"

"I don't know why not," he answered, pulling up on the reins. Ann and Kate scrambled down from the wagon and gathered the pungent, green leaves. Kate spied some mint growing in the shade and added it to the bunch.

"My, won't Ma be glad fer this," she beamed. "Hit makes the best drink with cold spring water."

Ann felt like wading in the clear water, but she knew it was much too cold this early in the year. As she walked along on the fragrant pine needles, she thought she would like to be a fairy and dance here under the soft pattern of sun and shade. Finally they drove to the hollow just below the Tate farm. All along the road grew Queen Anne's Lace and other early wild flowers. Such beauty amid such poverty, Ann thought. Yet the mountain people feared nature. They believed that God punished his children with hail, lightning, and drought.

As they pulled up to the cabin there did not seem to be anyone around. Not even the hound was there. Katie took this for a good sign.

"Guess Ma went off to visit," she lamented. She must be a sight better if she be gone."

"Don't feel bad, Katie," Ann consoled her. "We can come back again." Then setting down the basket of food, she added. "Let's leave everything on the porch for her. She will know we have been here."

"Thet's right," Katie agreed disappointedly. "Nobody but y'all would bring store coffee, so she'll be bound ter know it be we'uns. But hit do seem wrong fer Ma to be riding the wagon."

The drive back home was not pleasant. Ann hunted for something cheerful to talk about. "Katie," she finally began, "do you realize that in a few short weeks Tom will be coming home?"

"He shore will," Kate agreed, brightening a little. "Guess we'll go up to his ma's place and do up her work first. Have ye seen her lately, Preacher?" she asked, turning to John.

Frowning, John replied, "you know, I haven't. I should ride up there and check on her. Sure hope everything is all right. Usually I hear about her from someone every few days." Ann could feel the alarm in John's voice. She had been sure that Mrs. Matthews was fine, but now she had a chilling premonition. John also must have felt a real concern, for he did not turn the mare out. He fed and watered her in the stall, then hurried back into the cabin.

"Ann," he began, "there are still a few hours of light left, and I'll hurry. Please warm up some coffee, then I'll go and see about Tom's mother. I'll make it in by dark. Don't alarm Kate, but it's been too long since I have had any news of Mrs. Matthews."

"I'm glad you are going," Ann agreed. "I have a bad feeling that something is wrong. John, take care and watch out. Maybe that old woman is out to get us. I seem to see her face in the dark and once I know I heard her laugh." Ann turned away in confusion. Was she believing in the local superstitions?

"Now dear," John remonstrated, walking over and holding her against him. "You know God is on our side. Nothing is going to hurt you as long as you hold on to Him. You know, I have grown to love you more and more since we have been here," he said as he kissed her.

Confused, she turned away to get his coffee. Soon he rode up the trail and she stood, blinded by tears, and watched him ride out of sight. He wanted her to hold on to God. She didn't know how. But she could hold on to him and pray that nothing would happen to end this life. How could she ever have lived with a man like Bill and liked it? Still she wished she had the nice things she was used to. Looking at her hands she shuddered. Going to the mirror she saw her skin was not as soft and pretty as a year ago. I'll ask Aunt Cora to send creams and lotions, she thought. She wanted to keep her looks and figure in spite of all the other hardships. Someday they would be out of these back-woods and she did not want her friends to pity her. When Kate asked later where John was, Ann was evasive. She said he had ridden over to look at his fishing holes on Burnt Creek. That really wasn't a lie. He was sure to take a look as he rode by.

Chapter Thirteen

As John rode out of the clearing around the parsonage, he felt a cold wind rising. He hoped that he had left enough wood on the porch to keep the fire going. He would probably need to get in wood for Tom's mother when he got there, he reasoned, or she could need other help. Sawtooth Mountain was covered by a smoky, gray mantle, John noted. Some day he wanted to ride up to the top and see how it looked on the Missouri side.

Finally, he passed the ford on Burnt Creek. When he came within sight of the Matthew's split-rail fence, he saw the huge yellow cat again. This time the mare shied and John almost lost his balance. The cat arched its back and spat at him, then disappeared in the brush beside the trail. John sighed in relief and wondered again where the cat lived. He guessed it must be wild, and hoped he would not meet it again. Patting the mare's neck, he finally quieted her and started on toward the cabin. The late afternoon sun slanted through the pine and spruce trees, making a waving pattern on the dark, red boards under the cabin's eaves. It looked rustic, but with a little care it could be a pretty home. Even now the tangle of primrose, wild fern, and lilac, added a natural charm. As he tied the mare to the gate, he noticed an uneasy quiet.

He knocked on the door but there was no response. He knocked again and waited. Finally he tried the door and it opened. This was odd—John knew Tom's mother usually kept it barred. Inside, he could see the empty fireplace. There couldn't have been much of a fire in there today, he thought. Deciding to look around, he walked down the slope to the barn calling out for the hill woman. Only dead quiet answered him.

The barn was dark and smelled musty from wet hay. John forked some into the manger for the mule. Looking in the hen nests, he was surprised to find several eggs that had not been gathered. Becoming alarmed, he searched the barn but nothing else seemed wrong. Maybe she had gone off visiting on the mule. Then he remembered that she hated the mule. There was only one thing left for him to do. He would have to go back in the house and look around.

The back door seemed to be propped shut, so John went around to the front again. The Matthews cabin was large with two rooms and a long lean-to across the back, half of which was a kitchen, and the rest was Tom's room. Bedrooms opened off of the long living room on the north side. In the kitchen John saw the remains of a meal on the table. The stove was ice cold, so John knew nothing had been cooked that day. With mounting apprehension he went into the back bedroom and opened the curtains. The bed was empty and the quilt coverlet was in place. It looked dusty but was not out of order as far as John could tell. Uneasily he went to the other door, and paused. This must be Mrs. Matthews' room. Walking slowly in the dim light he raised the window shade. Then he saw her. She was propped up in bed with both pillows behind her. At first glance John thought that she was asleep—then he noticed her hair. Instead of being plaited in two long braids, it was cut close under her ears. Sara Matthews looked peaceful with her hands crossed on the covers.

In panic, John quickly backed out of the room and sat with shaking legs in one of the cane-bottomed chairs near the fireplace. After a minute or two he made himself go back in to be sure he had not been dreaming. Silently berating himself for being afraid, he took one of the cold hands in his and felt for a pulse. Only the rapid beat of his own heart filled his ears. Placing her arm in the exact position he had found it, he left the room and shut the door. Looking over the main room he could see no sign of any violence.

In his panic one thought was urgent: he must get word to Tom. Mounting the mare he hurried her out of the yard, trying to get away from the horror behind him. By now, the shadows were lengthening and the wind was becoming colder. John wished he had worn his heavy coat. What in the name of reason could have happened to her hair? He knew she would not have cut it, as long hair was the pride of every mountain woman. So why was it cut? He was taken by surprise again when the mare reared with him at a turn in the trail. This time he fell off and landed in a patch of brambles. Slightly dazed he could see the yellow eyes of the wild cat gleaming at him through the dusk.

"Ye'll larn someday to mind yer own business!" he heard a voice say. Already uncertain of his world and beliefs, John was doubting his sanity. Saying a brief prayer, he got up and started picking the briers out of his clothes. Was he just seeing things? He knew the cat was real—Ann had seen it too—still, cats do not speak. Rubbing his hurt shoulder he looked around for the mare. She was not there, and it was really dark now. Berating himself for being so stupid, he whistled. With relief he heard a faint nicker down the trail. At least he would not have to walk home. The rest of the way home he wondered how he could explain this to the girls without saying anything about Mrs.

Matthews' hair. He would just say that she had died in her sleep. Of course, by all that was holy, he thought of Granny Shook. Why would she want the hill woman's hair? Knowing he would have to ride on in to Gentry to phone the coroner, John tried to hurry the mare along. At home he found the two worried girls waiting with supper for him.

"Katie, Ann," he began once they were seated at the table, "I have bad news. I was right to be worried. I found Mrs. Matthews dead in her bed. She must have just died before I arrived."

A look of terror spread over Kate's face. Putting her head down on the table, her shoulders shook with sobs. "Oh Preacher, I knowed hit, I jest knowed some wicked thing was going to happen. And now my poor Tom will have to grieve and hit be all my fault. I feel like running clean out of here before old Granny gits after you folks too." Kate sat twisting her hands and rocking back and forth on the bench. Her long hair hung limp against her thin face and her eyes seemed hollow and staring. Oh God, don't let anything happen to Katie, Ann thought.

"Now Katie, I'm sure Mrs. Matthews has just died from natural causes," John remonstrated. "It could happen to anyone as old as she was." He could see Ann did not believe him.

"How'd she look?" Kate persisted. "Anything look strange at all about her?" She looked at John intently. "Ye might as well tell me 'cause I'll jest fine it out later on anyways."

Looking at the frightened girl across the table, John debated, then knew it was of no use to lie. It was not his nature to gloss over the truth. Living as he had been doing with Ann had been a hard strain. Pretending all was right, and not letting her know that he knew about her past had eaten like a canker into his mind.

"There was something quite strange," he admitted slowly. "All of Mrs. Matthew's hair had been cut off, right at her ears, and I did not see it lying around anywhere!"

"Oh God, thet shore sounds like Granny Shook's doings," Kate said. "Tom's ma had enough hair to last Granny fer years."

"Why in the world would she want Mrs. Matthews' hair?" Ann asked incredulously.

"Fer charms and such," Kate explained. "Lots of times they use the victim's own hair against them if they kin get a piece. And when a body cuts their fingernails, jest be good and sure and throw them in the fire."

Ann shuddered and turned to John. "We must get word to Tom right away. What a shock this will be to him, and right at examination time too."

"The mare is exhausted and so am I. But it will be better to go now than early in the morning. As for this nonsense about witches and charms, I want you girls to promise to get it out of your mind. There must be a logical reason for her hair being cut and Tom probably will know," John stated. "I don't want you two to leave this cabin until I get back."

"Won't do a mite of good if'n thet old womern takes a notion ter come in," Kate stated. "But I dare say she be a long way from here by now."

John thought of and started to mention his second encounter with the cat that had just occurred, but decided to keep quiet about it. Ann was nervous enough already. Taking his coat and a lantern, he went out to the tired mare. "Sorry old girl," he apologized, "but you have one more ride to make this night."

It was a miserable trip through the dark night—the cold wind was at his back and his shoulder was throbbing. Perhaps he should have confided in Ann so she could have rubbed liniment on it. When he arrived in Gentry, John was relieved to see that Yancey had not put out his light and gone to bed. He found the big man fooling around with his crystal radio. At first he told John he had just picked up Denver and offered him the headphones, not noticing John's tired face. John sadly told him what had happened and waited while Yancey put the call through to Tom. He was hoping that Rose had not heard what he said. It seemed like hours before they finally got Tom on the phone.

"Tom, you must come home right away," John told him gravely. "Your mother has died in her sleep. I went up there this afternoon and it looked like she had only been dead a few hours. If you can make it home in the morning, we could bury her before night."

"Preacher, that's sure bad news," Tom answered slowly. "I thought Ma was in good shape when I left. Did Katie see her? It sure does seem sudden, Preacher. I think I can catch a truck to Gentry. Can you call the coroner and make the arrangements for me? Maybe Bud will make her a box. It just don't seem real that Ma is gone." Tom's voice faltered and John almost thought the line had gone dead. Then back came his voice. "I sure do thank you, Preacher," he finally said. "I'll be there soon as I can."

The phone went dead and as the hollow sound assailed him, John felt so sorry for Tom. It was almost time for his spring exams and now he would have to come home to face this sorrow. Turning to Yancey, John asked if he had the number of the coroner in Siloam.

"It's written right here on the wall, John," the big man said. "Would you like me to make the call for you?"

"I sure would," John said, obviously very relieved. "I'd like to get back as soon as I can." Turning, he hesitated, "Mr. Yancey, why would Mrs. Matthews have her hair cut off? She was lying peacefully in her bed, but all of her hair was cut right off under her ears."

"Well," Yancey replied, evading the question, "that's going to stir up a lot of trouble. We have enough feuding and fussing here already without witchcraft starting up again. Guess somebody still has it in for Kate. Of course everybody will blame this on Granny Shook. Between you and me, John, she's capable of about any mean thing you could name. Just looking into that old woman's eyes gives me the shakes."

"Why, Yancey," John exclaimed, "I didn't think you believed in superstitions!"

"After you've lived around here as long as I have, you may believe them too," the big man replied defensively. "I tell you, I've seen a lot of strange things in these hills. Things that there was no logical reason for. I have seen a whole barn full of milk cows dry up overnight, two of them with new calves. I heard a young woman accuse another woman of following after her man. She threatened to put a spell on her hens so they would stop laying. And by God, they quit too! I know it sounds like foolishness, but I know what I seen."

"I just can't believe in witchcraft," John protested. "I know there are many places in the Bible that says some people have divers spirits, but I haven't known of any cases in these days."

"Don't see why there can't be the same things possible now as in the old times," Yancey argued. "I sure know the old devil operates in these hills, and I bet he can count on plenty of helpers. John, I wouldn't have your job for a thousand dollars. Anyway, we'd better get the call through. It'll take Mr. Brown half a day to ride up here. Think Tom will want to lay her beside his father in the old cemetery?"

"That's the only place close around," John speculated. "I doubt he would bury her on their farm. I will have to go get Bud early in the morning to see about his making a coffin. Does he do this for all of the people?"

"For about everyone around that I know of if they can't do it themselves," Yancey replied. "Not many have the price for one out of Siloam. About all these people can manage to do is eat and keep a roof over their heads. I wanted to sell out and leave after my first year here, but couldn't get my money out of the business, so Rose and I had to stay. Now I've grown to like the people and I feel that I've helped them by my running the store. None of them can make the sixteen miles to Siloam, but at least they can get this far to buy necessities. I try to carry what staples and medicines they need to meet most emergencies. What we need most is a doctor. Many a child has died because folks couldn't get to a doctor."

"That's what I hope Tom will be," John said. "It seems that the Lord has a hand in that boy's life. I think He wants him to come back here and practice."

"I sure hope so," Yancey agreed. "Well, John, I hope this don't start up any more trouble. I'll send old Brown over and you can ride up with him. You and Bud or Jess can lay her out when the coffin is ready." Yancey paused and looked at John curiously. "Aren't you just a little nervous keeping Kate at the parsonage?"

"No, she can stay until Tom is able to take her with him," he stated firmly.

Riding home in the cold, he thought about what Yancey had said. Could it be possible that this could be the devil's work? He had to admit that many strange things had been happening in the year he had been here. He decided to search his Bible for references about spirits and witches. Then he remembered the cat and began to pay strict attention to the mare and the trail.

When John finally got home, Ann was sound asleep. She had left the lamp burning and the coffeepot warming on the back of the stove. Wearily John prepared for a few hours rest. At first light he was up and, without breakfast, saddling the mare once again. He left Ann a note and started up to the Childer's place.

Bud reacted as John had thought he would. Effie was just as vehement as she informed him how she felt.

"Tain't no surprise to we'uns. They should run thet old she-cat clean over into Missouri. They's jest what they did once to the old womern that was hanging 'round Price's mill a few yars back."

"Now Effie, you shet up," Bud warned, looking around warily. "They say old Granny can hear for miles around. Anyway, I'd best git up and round up some boards. May have to borrow around. Preacher, do you want ter go along?"

"No, Bud, I have to go home and wait for the coroner. I have to take him up to the Matthews' place. When the coffin is ready bring it on over to Mrs. Matthews'. Tom should make it here by tonight. We'll have to bury her by tomorrow at the latest."

"Ye hain't going ter bring her inter the meeting house, Preacher?" Effie asked in alarm.

"Of course we will," John replied in surprise. "She must have a decent service."

"Hit ain't right, Preacher," Bud stated flatly. "We'uns had best jest take the box out to whar we dig the hole and let ye say yer piece." He finished his coffee in one nervous gulp. "We'uns don't want our meeting house witched too."

Angry and surprised, John choked back his reply, deciding not to press the issue. He intended to hold Mrs. Matthews' funeral in the church no matter what they said.

He arrived back home about noon and found the girls at the cabin. After taking care of the mare, he found the shovel and carried it up to the back porch. He told them he had to help dig the grave as soon as he got through with the coroner.

"Oh no," Kate objected. "Ye cain't dig it 'til tomorrow. Ye best not leave thet hole open all night, that be jest asking fer more trouble."

Ann and John exchanged glances. Ann was more frightened by the terror in Katie's voice so John gave in.

"Alright, Kate, I'll talk to Tom when he gets here. I'm sure we will have time in the morning." Personally, he could not see what difference it could make if the hole stood empty. He had seen graves dug several days before a funeral. This poor, superstitious girl really believed what she had said. Now she had Ann worried too. It would be a wonder if she ever believed in anything he stood for in this heathen place.

It was after lunch when Coroner Brown arrived. He was a little, balding man, in a shiny, black suit. After offering him something to eat, John rode with him to the Matthews' place. John thought he could see wheel tracks in the yard and wondered who could have been there. They started in the front door after John explained he had left it unbarred.

Making their way into the bedroom, they found Mrs. Matthews exactly as John had left her. Looking her over carefully, Mr. Brown said he could see no cause of death other than natural causes. However, he did look curiously at her shorn head.

"We can't understand that either," John commented. "She had long hair, usually done up in a knot on top of her head. I can't imagine why she would have cut it off."

"Well, about anything can happen in these hills, and does," the coroner informed him. "Many strange things have happened that I have seen, with no logical explanation. I try to ignore them if possible and see they have a proper burial. You say someone is bringing a coffin? You will have to sign a statement saying you found her here yesterday," he added.

After talking to the coroner at length, John was relieved. Soon, they heard the crunch of wagon wheels and Bud drove in with the pine box. When they laid her out, Bud whistled through his teeth and turned sharply to John.

"This here beats all I ever did see!" he exclaimed. "Somebody shore give her a shearing. We'd best hunt fer a bonnet fer her. No use setting the holler to talking." He rummaged in a chest, found a ruffled cap, and placed it on Mrs. Matthews' head. Once he had tied the bow neatly under her chin, only a few straggling, red hairs showed. Nobody could see that her hair had been cut.

"Now she looks more natural like," Bud stated. Laying a thick blanket in the coffin, they straightened her body out inside. Bud drove a couple of nails in the top to help hold it for the ride back. "We'd best jest leave her on the wagon 'til Tom comes and we get the hole dug," he suggested.

"No, Bud, now we will go on to the church and have a decent service." John spoke as firmly as he could.

"Wal, hev it yore own way, Preacher, but hit ain't no place fer hit," Bud argued. "Besides, she ain't going to smell good at all by tomorrow."

Looking at Coroner Brown, John noticed a faint smile and commented that he might not have very many mourners attend the service.

Tom did not reach Yancey's store until dark. John was waiting there for him with the wagon. Stowing Tom's suitcase in the back, he brought him up to date.

"Guess it's up to you and me to dig her grave in the morning," he told the saddened young man.

"Yes," Tom answered slowly. "She's already laid too long. It's a good thing it is still cold weather. Do you believe she'd been dead very long before you found her?" he asked curiously.

"The coroner said he thought not much over twenty-four hours when he examined her," John explained. "The stove was cold and I expect she had just laid down early."

"I wonder, Preacher," Tom answered uneasily. "At any rate, she is dead. I thought Ma was feeling good when I left. With her hair cut that way, it don't look good to me. But the less said, the better. I think I might as well tell you that I've decided to come back here to live some day, and try to take care of these people."

"You don't know how happy that makes me," John enthused. "That is the best news I have heard in a long time. You are certainly needed and I know people around here will be happy to have you for their doctor."

"I'm not so sure about that, Preacher," Tom said uncertainly. "You see, they are all so sure Katie is a bad girl and witched that they may be afraid of me, too. But if we stay away while I finish school, maybe folks will forget."

"It's going to be a hard grind for you, Tom. I know that you have the determination to see it through." John felt a wave of sympathy for the weary boy.

Early the next morning the two men dug the grave. The soil was rich and loamy underneath the trees behind the church. John had always wondered why the cemetery was so full of weeds. Apparently nobody took care of it. Tom explained that most of the men were afraid of the dead and wanted no part of caring for graves.

"I have tended my father's grave more than most do," he added, "but for the last few years I have neglected it too. You see, it seems I just never had enough time after I finished all of the chores that Ma wanted me to do."

John decided to take Bud's advice and bury Mrs. Matthews without a service inside the church. As he read a few verses over the pine casket, he saw that there were few mourners. At least Bud, Hattie, and Jess were there. As he and Bud shoveled the last spade of dirt on the mound, Hattie placed a little vase of wild flowers. Tom added a little pine cross marked her name on it: Sarah Lowe Matthews; Born 1869; Died April 5, 1922. In the adjoining grave lay Tom's father, Lawrence Matthews. After he read the headstone, John suddenly realized how young Tom had been when his father had died in 1909. He could understand now how Mrs. Matthews must have felt to have her only son leave.

The Childers and Hattie withdrew to their wagons and waited for Tom and Katie to say their last farewells. Looking around, John saw, with alarm, the big yellow cat crouched at the edge of the clearing, watching the proceedings with big, luminous eyes. Hoping the others would not see, he hurried Ann back to their wagon. In a few minutes Tom and Kate joined them and they rode in silence back to the parsonage.

"When be ye going back to school?" Hattie asked Tom.

"I'll have to go back tomorrow," Tom told her, noticing the disappointed look on Katie's face. "I have two tests to make up as it is. After that I'll be able to come home in two weeks. I hope to have a few days of work for the school, getting the buildings closed for the summer."

"That time will pass before you know it," Ann told Kate.

"But he jest got here, Miss Ann," Kate cried. "Hit jest don't seem fair."

"I know," Tom comforted her. "But I'll be able to take you with me this fall." His dark face matched the smile on Kate's. "It will be a lot better having you there with me."

"It may be better for you," Ann complained, "but not for us. It's been like having a sister with Katie here this past winter."

"Hev ye got hit all set, this being a doctor?" Jess asked him.

"Sure have," Tom stated firmly. "I'm going to be the best family doctor in all these hills." He smiled at them with a renewed determination.

"We'uns shore could use a doc," Hattie told him. "And I jest know Tom will make a good one. Your Ma will see ye even if ye cain't see her. The spirits be all around us, Tom."

"You mean the dead are not asleep in the earth?" Ann asked in surprise.

"I know they hain't. I done seen my old grandma onc't. She warned me not to walk down into the 'mater patch. Jess found a big spreadnanner jest waiting fer me." Hattie's face was grim. "He'd a got me for shore. Lots of folks here git bit and some die. I cain't do much for pizen. We shore need a doctor."

"They all run after Hattie fer everything from babies to warts," Jess declared. "Many a long night she takes keer of folks, then comes home to take keer of Lettie May and me."

"I know it's true," Tom responded. "I only hope I can be as good and kind so people will trust me like they do you Hattie."

"Hit will come, Tom. Folks will larn ter trust ye. Jest wait and ye'll see," she replied.

"I'll take you in to Gentry in the morning," Jess offered. The kind, hill man added as an afterthought, "Kate, ye kin ride along if'n ye be a'mind to."

"That would help, Jess," Tom replied gratefully. "The earlier I'm there the more I might get a ride on to Siloam."

After the Childers left, Ann went out under a tree to be alone. The young people were talking in the kitchen and John was caring for the mare. If the dead were all around, they certainly knew all about her. She hoped they knew how hard she was trying. Once again she prayed that her past would never catch up with her and that Bill would never find his way here. She was just now learning to love this place.

⚜ Chapter Fourteen ⚜

The next morning Kate and Tom left with Jess in his wagon as the sun cast its first rays into the hollow. As she watched from the front window, Ann knew that this was a scene that would soon be repeated for good. Turning resolutely away she tackled the morning chores. "No use worrying before I have to," she announced firmly to the dirty dishes. John was on one of his calling trips and was not due back until late afternoon. As she was making the bed she was startled to hear a horse ride in. John couldn't be home by now, she thought. Running into the kitchen she looked out to see Bill. In a sudden panic she ran to her bedroom and smoothed her hair. She looked in vain for her rouge, pinched her cheeks, threw off her apron and put on her pretty mules. A brisk knock shocked her into action and she flew to the door.

"Annie, let me in. I know you are home… I met your friends on their way to town," he said. Pushing open the door, he quickly held her trembling body close. Ann thought she might faint from the current between them. Pushing him away with all of her strength, she sat in one of the kitchen chairs.

Bill's intense, dark eyes bored right through her.

"God, Annie, how could you leave me? We really had something, you know it. If it is marriage you want, come on back and we can do it. Now that I have found you, I won't let you go." His flushed face showed his passion; his dark, wavy hair was perfectly combed. Even after riding five miles on a horse, his neat, grey suit looked fresh.

"Bill, you don't know what you are saying. I love my life here, and I have the most loving and fine man I have ever known." These were not the words she wanted to say to him, but she had learned a lot about morals the past few months.

"Annie, I don't believe you," he argued, trying to put his arms around her again. Afraid of his strength and passion, she decided to try another approach.

"Come on, let's go for a walk down by the creek," she said and took his hand. "You know, we never did much talking, did we? I don't believe you ever gave me a chance to tell you what I wanted out of life."

Quickly changing her shoes again, she led him down the path all the while keeping up a lively, nervous chatter. She talked of the natives, their odd ways, and about helping with Jennie's baby until they heard the gurgle of Burnt Creek. Suddenly Bill pulled her down on the grassy slope, his mouth burning against hers. Ann willed herself not to respond. Holding her lips tight she almost succeeded. As if from habit he reached down, unbuttoned her blouse, and began fondling her breast. Then, against her will, her emotions and the old magic of the man engulfed her. Holding his head in her hands, she gave caress for caress, finding his kiss like a fire, deep within her.

"Oh Annie, I have dreamed of finding you. Your aunt was no help. I found out from your mailman in Denver. He said your letters came from Gentry, so I hired a horse. I have tried to replace you with other girls, but there is nobody like you, Annie."

"This isn't right, Bill. Our love is all in the past. We can't begin again. I could never hurt John. It's true you bring out the passion in me, but he means more to me than just a bed partner."

"You know he can't love you like I can. God, you set me on fire," and his lips brushed hers. Amid his caresses her senses whirled. She knew John was a poor match for this man. Bill knew all of the ways to thrill a woman. Thinking of him loving others since she had been gone made her ache. Holding him tighter, it seemed she could not get her fill of him. How could she have left a man like this?

Spent from passion, she lay in his arms and gazed through the leafy canopy above them. Pale shafts of sunlight filtered through to the forest floor. Feeling his arms tighten around her once more, she was again lost in his embrace. It was then that she felt a cold, chilling presence. Trying to pull away, she heard a taunting laugh.

"Heh, heh, now I got ye!"

Ann knew it was the old crone, but where was she? The spell was broken, she hurriedly got to her feet and brushed the leaves from her dress and hair. Bill jumped up and tried to take her in his arms again.

"What is it Annie? Don't pull away. I'll never let you go again," he said. Ann evaded him, her heart was burning.

"I'll never leave John. He is by far a better man. You got what you came for: you're convinced no woman can resist you and I guess it is true. I once thought I couldn't live without you, but now all I feel is contempt. Why, half the time I lived with you, you were cheating." His handsome face dominated her senses.

"Annie, you can't mean that. How can you turn away from a love like ours? This life isn't for you. Look at your hands... your hair needs care, and your face isn't the lovely, soft face I kissed before. How can you stand this place? We really had something, I thought you were happy and I don't see why you left."

"Bill, please! If I ever meant anything to you, go away. I don't want John to ever find out what a bad person he has married. He thinks I'm so good—I've tried to be good—but now you've made me forget everything. Please, please… go back to Denver and leave me alone."

"Why fight me, Annie," he responded. "You know you can't kiss me and still tell me to go." Drawing her to him he pressed his lips on hers. Ann steeled her mind to resist. She thought of the hurt look in John's face and was able not to respond. Slowly Bill released her, his handsome face scowling. A white line around his mouth told Ann of his anger.

"Come on and get your horse," Ann called as she ran back up the trail. "I want you to leave before Katie gets back." Ann did not look back until she came out of the trees by the road. Then, walking more lady-like, she saw that John had not returned. When she made it to the back porch, she saw that Bill was coming and Katie was waiting by the door.

"Miss Ann, do ye know who's horse this be?"

"Yes, Katie, it is a friend of mine. I have been showing him the creek. He has to hurry back to Denver. How long have you been here?"

"Oh, we must have met yer friend. He was asking me and Jess about ye. Cain't he stay and meet the preacher?" Kate watched curiously as Bill untied his horse from the porch rail.

"No, Katie, come on and don't say anything. Let him go on. I don't want to talk to him anymore." Drawing the young girl into the kitchen, Ann shut the door firmly. She could see Bill standing irresolute beside his mount. Inwardly she prayed he would hurry. What if John rode in?

"Annie, you know I don't give up easily," he finally called out. "I'll give you a few more weeks and then I'm coming back. You can count on it!" Mounting with his customary grace, he swung the horse out on the trail. With a sigh of relief Ann saw him disappear behind the trees. Falling into a chair, she buried her face in her hands. What had she done? She had forgotten about Kate and was startled by the hill girl's concern.

"Miss Ann, what be the matter? Did that man hurt ye? What be the matter, Miss Ann?"

"I used to think I loved that man, Katie. Please don't tell anyone he was here. Oh Katie, I have been such a fool! He isn't anything compared to John. I used to dream about his fine home, and all of the luxuries there. But they can't compare to what I have here. Please, Katie, promise me you won't tell John."

"Ye don't need to worry on my account, but Jess may say he saw this feller," Kate said doubtfully to Ann.

"We'll just wait and see. Let's get started on dinner now and try not to worry," she answered. "John promised to take us to see your mother, so we need to bake up some good things to take to her."

As the shadows lengthened, Ann began to worry again. John should have returned by now and after hearing the menacing words of the old woman, Ann did not want to be alone with only Kate. Had she imagined that awful laugh? Her thoughts went wild as she set the table. It was with great relief that she heard John ride into the shed. John burst in with news of his own.

"I heard today that your father is down in bed," he told Kate. "I was told he had sent to Yancey's for herbs to make tea." He hesitated, then went on. "Katie, if he is down in bed he can't chase us away. We wanted to go see your mother anyway, so let's go in the morning."

"I'd shore like thet, Preacher. I been saving some ginseng from last year in my trunk. I could take it to him. I bet thet would make him better, but then," she added lamely, "he's apt to be afraid ter take herbs from me."

When supper was finally over, Ann rose in relief. It had been a real strain, and she had found it hard to meet John's gaze. Surely he must suspect something.

That night, as she lay beside John her body quivered remembering Bill's embrace. Praying John would turn over and go to sleep, she lay rigid. There was no way she could love him tonight. Soon she heard his even breathing and knew she had won reprieve. It was far into the night before she could settle her mind. Once she thought she heard footsteps. Trying to tell herself it had all been a bad dream, she finally found rest.

⚜ Chapter Fifteen ⚜

When they arrived at the Tate cabin the next morning, a worried Lucy opened the door and met them out on the porch. She sobbed and threw her arms around Katie.

"Honey, hit shore is a treat to see ye. Many be the times I prayed fer ye to come, and pleaded with yer pa to send word. I heared all about the poor little young'un."

"Ma, Ma, I wanted to see ye so bad. I ain't never agin going to stay away so long." Peering into the kitchen she asked, "How be Pa?"

"Wal, he's down whar he cain't do much harm," the frail woman said with relief. "But, Preacher," turning to John, "I'd shore like fer ye to go in and talk to him fer a spell."

Taking John through the front room into the back, she began to elaborate. "He shore don't look good a'tall. I shore wish we'uns had a doctor in these parts. You know he's been riled up fer a long spell."

"I know," John agreed. "I hope I won't make him more so." Walking into the darkened room, he could barely see the old man in the big four-poster bed. Eli opened his eyes and seemed to be trying to sit up when he saw John.

"Now lie still and don't get excited, Mr. Tate," John advised. "I heard you were not well, and came to see if I could be of any help to you."

"Don't want no help from the likes of ye. Cain't see why ye air here no how. Never sent fer ye and I ain't fixing to die jest yet." The old man was rigid with hate as he shouted loudly and beat his bony hands against the covers.

"Of course you aren't going to die," John agreed. "None of us ever want to die. We heard you were down in bed, and felt we should come. Also Katie wanted to see her mother."

"She ain't got no claim on her ma no more. She done made her bed hard, now jest let her lay in hit. Sin always gits ye, Preacher, and that Kate be a sinner. Don't want her on this place, so ye jest take her on back and keep her away from here!" Eli's white hair seemed to stand on end, and his face grew red from anger.

"I'm sorry to hear you still feel bitter, Mr. Tate," John despaired. "Your wife wants to talk to Katie, so we must stay for a little while."

"No ye won't nuther," the old man screamed and tried to get up out of the bed. The effort was too much for him and he sank back on the pillow. In alarm John watched his face turn ashen and called to Lucy.

"I told ye, Preacher, thet he'd have a fit. Stubborn as a Missouri mule, Eli be. Ye'd best be still, Eli. Katie is here to see ye too. So you tell her ye forgive her a'fore ye die with meanness in your soul!" The little hill woman was suddenly brave as her tormenter lay still in the bed.

Katie looked with surprise at her mother, so did Ann and John. Something had happened to the meek mother Katie had always known. Eli closed his lips tight and then turned his face to the wall. Finally, everyone walked silently out of the room.

"Here, take ye a cup of coffee and some apple cobbler ter go home on. Eli hain't going to do ye no harm. The good Lord done put him down fer a spell," Lucy said. Her brown eyes crinkled and Ann could tell she was glad to have this freedom at last. "And Kate, I mean fer ye and Tom to come see me when he gits back. I been a'heering about him going ter that big school. I be right proud ter have him fer kin. Ye'll have a right smart life, and ye won't jest be hoeing taters and raising a passel of young'uns nuther."

"Ma, Tom's aiming to be a doctor," Katie told her eagerly. "Now ain't it a sight!"

"Hit shore is," Lucy agreed. "Jest think, we'uns will have our own doctor right here in our own holler. Seems jest too good ter be true. My, Katie, won't ye be proud! They won't be a'talking agin ye when ye be the doctor's wife."

"Ma, have ye seen or heerd tell of Granny lately?" Katie asked.

"Shore hain't, Kate," Lucy answered. "When yer pa got down in bed, she jest up and disappeared right sudden like. I thought she war out in the lean-to, but when I called her to come eat, she warn't nowhere around. Have ye seen her?" she asked, turning around to John and Ann.

"No, Mrs. Tate," John replied, "but we did hear she was up around Sawtooth with a family beyond the mill. It is a family I have not met yet. They are too far to come to Sunday services."

"I don't rightly know jest who them folks be, but I shore feel right sorry fer them if thet old womern is up thar," Lucy declared earnestly.

"Why, Ma, I thought ye held with Granny!" Kate exclaimed, looking at her mother closely.

"Not me, it war yer Pa done fetched her when he got so het up at ye and some others here. He shore knows hit be wrong ter fool with the devil's doings. Now he be paying fer having took with her, and he knows hit."

"We will keep praying for Eli," John promised. "And I will come back again soon and try to talk with him. Maybe if Kate is not along he won't get so mad."

"Hit won't do ary bit of good," Lucy complained. "Thet thar man is the stubbornest old fool I ever did see. He hain't going ter admit ever thet he be wrong."

"Hit won't hurt fer the preacher to try, Ma," Kate remonstrated. "Ma, do ye need anything?" she inquired. "We'uns could tote hit from Gentry. Who be doing the chores?"

"Why I been taking keer of the stock myself," Lucy told her with pride. "And I still got plenty of coffee and sugar. I be jest about out of snuff though."

"Ye shore got better mighty sudden like," Kate questioned. "I cain't understand hit."

"It war strange," Lucy admitted. "My old bones had been hurting bad all winter, but ye know," turning to face John, "soon as thet old womern left, I got right over hit. Ye know, Preacher, the old devil shore can pull a body down if'n he wants."

"That is true, Mrs. Tate," John agreed. "The power of the devil is so great that we can't imagine it. I am glad you are up. Katie has been so worried. If you need help or if Eli gets worse let me know."

"Tain't nuthing bad the matter I reckon," Lucy said. "Hit be mostly that he be a prideful man, and he thinks he cain't hold up his head now down at the store on account of Kate." Then she added as an afterthought, "Watch out fer thet old womern. I jest know she be after ye."

"Ma, take keer of yerself, and we'll git ye the snuff," Kate promised as they drove away.

All the way home Ann could hear that eerie laugh and the old woman's words. What had she meant that now she had Ann?

Surely she would not find a way to tell John that she had been making love with Bill. After the tales she had heard here she knew it was possible. God, she thought, just give me another chance and I will never get out of line again. What a nerve she had praying to God when she wasn't sure there was a God at all. She must be losing her mind. Glancing up at John she realized what a wonderful man he was. Don't ever find me out, she thought. She could not bear to see the hurt in his blue eyes. Seeing Kate look at her wondering, she masked her emotions the rest of the way home.

⊰ Chapter Sixteen ⊱

The following Saturday morning while Ann was sweeping the back porch, she noticed an old hornet nest under the rafters and knocked it down with the broom. The large, round object bounced down and lay at her feet, dusty and dry. She moved back quickly, expecting to be stung, but soon realized that the nest was not being used. Ann swept it out into the yard and continued on with her chore. When Katie saw it laying there, her face tightened.

"Whar did thet thang come from?" she asked.

"I knocked down from the wall when I was sweeping this morning," Ann explained.

"I wonder if hit war put thar a'purpose," Kate said. "Hit's shore funny I never did see hit before."

"It's just an old hornet nest," Ann smiled.

"May be, but them things air suspicious. Could be fer you, and then hit could be fer me. Hope hit be fer you and the preacher. Tom and I shore don't need no young'un fer a long time. Leastways not till he gits ter be a doctor."

"Well, if that's what all this means, I hope it is meant for me too," Ann replied. "Let's put it back quick." Ann gingerly picked up the mud nest and tried to reach up to the ceiling, but the rafter was too high. So, she laid it in a chink in the log.

"Wouldn't hit be good fer ye and the preacher. I bet he'd jest have a fit he'd be so glad," Katie went on.

"Katie, don't say anything to John," Ann cautioned. "He doesn't believe in these superstitions and I'm not so sure I do either. Besides, we have to wait and be sure."

"I purely won't, Miss Ann," Katie promised, "but I jest wish I knew which of us thet thang was meant fer."

Ann was thinking the same thing and found that now she had another worry: what if she was the one? How would she know for sure it would be John's child? Oh God, that must have been what the old witch was laughing about. What a fool she had been! She could bear anything if he just never found out. Now her punishment seemed more than she could stand.

On most Sundays the little church was usually only half full. This always made John feel sad to realize that even though he visited all of the families for miles around, he was not fully accepted here. Things moved slowly in these hills. He thought that the shipment of trees he had ordered for Holcomb would spark their interest. He wanted so much to find a cash crop for these people. So many things were needed here, and he prayed he could make life easier. He tried to put his own doubts and unhappiness aside and do the work he had been sent here to do.

On the Sunday after their visit to the Tates' Ann felt a current running through the small congregation. As they sang "Bringing In The Sheaves" the words rolled out like a folk song, with much tapping of feet. She doubted any of them really understood the meaning. Hattie & Jess were in their customary seats and Effie and Bud had their three children with them.

John had just started his sermon when Ann heard a horse

and rider outside. The back door opened gently, and an unshaven, dark, young man in a crumpled, black hat slid into the back pew. John hesitated, then went on with his preaching.

When Lettie May had finished playing the last hymn, John walked to the back door to shake hands with the people as they left. Hattie and Jess recognized the stranger immediately.

"Why, Tad Price!" Hattie called out. "What in the world air ye doing in the meeting house?"

"Got ter see the preacher," the young man replied shortly, turning toward John.

"Preacher, I hain't fit ter be here asking no favors. I been a sinner all my days, but the Lord knows I hain't never lied nor stole from no man, and I shore do need ye to help me and my pa in the worst way."

"Tad, we're all sinners. That is why I came here to live in the first place. I want to help all of you. Now tell me what is your trouble?" John gently eased the distraught young man into a pew and Ann drew the others out the door. She could see that Bud was bursting with curiosity and knew that he would not leave until he knew what was going on.

"My pa," Ann heard the stranger saying, "he's right bad off. He cain't talk a'tall, and we'uns think somebody done pizened him. Why Preacher, he cain't even stand up!"

"Have you called on anyone else for help?" John asked. "Do you think we should take him to Gentry and call a doctor from Siloam? Maybe Hattie could help, or know what is the matter with him. When did this happen?"

"It jest come on yesterday. And Pa cain't go clear down to Gentry, he cain't even set up! We'uns heered ye ain't a'feered of old Granny. Pa made her mad up to the mill. She jest lit out up to Lundys' place over t'other side of Sawtooth. Then Pa was took real bad." Tears filled Tad's eyes and he dabbed at them in shame.

"Tad, I don't know what I can do," John answered. "You know

I'm not a doctor but I will go with you to see him. I feel Hattie could do more though." John was puzzled by the boy's insistence and knew he must go.

"We'uns want ye should come and git rid of old Granny's spell, like ye did fer Kate." Tad turned and looked fearfully out the back door.

"All I can do, Tad, is pray for your father. This I will be happy to do. In fact, I'll get ready right now. You wait while I saddle the mare." Turning to Bud he told him matter-of-factly, "Bud, I have to go up to the mill. Tad's father is feeling bad and wants to see me." Ann admired his coolness in the face of all of the curiosity in everyone waiting.

"Fix up a lunch, Ann," he requested. "It's quite a ride and I am sure Tad is hungry already. We should hurry too." Ann saw Hattie and the Childers talking out by their wagons and knew that they had heard some of what Tad had said. Telling them all good-bye she hurried Kate into the parsonage.

"Oh my," Kate lamented. "Now our fine cooking fer our Sunday dinner be all wasted. Guess we can put the chicken and fried pies in their lunch though."

"Nothing will be wasted," Ann laughed. "It looks to me that Tad needs some home cooking."

"Oh, he probably drinks enough moonshine to keep a'going ye can bet," Kate informed her. "Him and his pa been running a still up back of the mill fer a right long time."

"You mean they make whiskey?" Ann asked in surprise, "I thought the government stopped that years ago. I remember reading that they had closed down all of the illicit stills."

"Maybe they closed down some," Kate said, "but they'll never stop all of them in these hills. Not as long as there be any corn thet's growing."

"I sure hope John doesn't get mixed up in any trouble like that," Ann worried. "I hope he doesn't meet up with that old

woman either. We better put out a blanket. He might not be able
to get back till tomorrow."

John was worrying about moonshine, too, and wondered if
old man Price had simply had too much of his own brew to
drink. He had heard accounts of drunken fights up at the mill.
As he and Tad set out, a chill wind cut through the pines,
although it was late May. Tad rode silently until John offered
him some of the fried chicken.

"Guess I am right hongry, Preacher," the lanky boy con-
fessed, his eyes lighting up at the sight of the crusty, brown
drumstick. "Don't rightly recollect if'n I had any grub at all
since yesterday."

"Tad, where are your brothers?" John asked. "It seems to me
that I met two of them at the store."

"Wall," Tad answered, wiping his mouth on his sleeve, "Jeb,
he be over to Missouri fer a spell. He done got in a fight over a
womern and had to light out. Burl, he comes and goes. Guess
you know what fer, without me telling ye."

"Isn't it risky selling whiskey, Tad?" John questioned. "I've
heard that government men come through here every once in
awhile looking for moonshiners. Haven't they ever come up
around Sawtooth?"

"Yep, they shore hev," Tad grinned. "My grandpap got shot
once, but Pa, now he's a heap smarter. Cain't nobody but him
find his workings." John noticed that Tad spoke with pride.
"Course if'n he cain't git ter walking agin, he just might be
obliged to tell me whar hit be."

"But Tad," John persisted, "don't you make enough running
the mill? Do you need to make whiskey too?"

"Shore, but mill work is a lot harder and Pa says moonshining is a lot more fun. Leastwise thet be what Pa says," Tad mum-
bled. "Pa makes good likker," he added defensively. "Thar be
some kinds that will dang near kill a man. Them thieving,

no-good Lundys make some thet hain't fit fer the hogs." Tad spit angrily at the scrub pine along the trail. "They sure as shooting told old Granny to hex my pa so he cain't make no more."

John was strongly tempted to discount this, but after what he had seen happen, he kept silent. He could not overcome superstitions with arguments. He thought about asking Tad if he had seen the yellow cat, but decided against it.

The wind came on stronger as the sun dropped behind Sawtooth and the two men climbed higher and higher. The pines were thicker now, moaning as they swayed in the wind. The mill itself was off to the left of Burnt Creek, but the Price cabin was several hundred feet higher up on the mountain. Tad dismounted, tied his horse, and indicated a tree for John to use for his mare. Together they climbed the last few yards on foot. Ducking to enter the small door, Tad motioned John to follow. As John tried to adjust his eyes to the gloom, Tad lit the lamp.

"Guess Pa be sleeping," Tad observed. As the flickering lamp burned brighter, John saw the gaunt, old man on a bunk, his long hair almost white partially covering his face. But the old man was far from being asleep. His eyes were like a cornered animal, intently watching the two men. John thought he saw disapproval in his face and figured he resented him being there.

"Pa, I done fetched the preacher," Tad said, kneeling beside the bunk. "Pa, he can shore git rid of old Granny's spell." Turning to John, he added sadly, "See, I told ye he cain't talk a'tall. Cain't ye do something, Preacher?"

John felt at a complete loss. He took the old man's limp hand in his, then felt of his forehead. It didn't feel like he had a fever. Wishing he knew a little more about medicine, he decided to do what he knew the best, pray. Looking into the old man's wary eyes, he began.

"Dear God, you know all about Mr. Price here. You know what his condition is and what has caused it. We are all your children and in a state of sin. Tad has said that he is a sinner and he needs your help. Mr. Price can't ask for help, Lord, but I feel sure he knows you are able to help him, and wants to be forgiven. Lord, I put him in your hands and ask in Jesus' name that you help him back to his normal health. In your will, Amen." John remained on his knees for a few moments before looking up at the old man. When he did he saw that Price's eyes were closed. Fearing that he might be dead, he felt his pulse and was relieved to find a steady beat.

"He seems to have dropped off to sleep, Tad," John said. "Maybe he will be better when he awakens."

"I shore do hope so," Tad answered guardedly. "I wish Jeb or Burl war home. I never been alone since Ma has been gone. Pa's always been the boss. Taught me how to mill, but he never showed none of us how to run the still. He lets Burl peddle the likker all over, even down to Missouri."

"You are better off not knowing," John reassured him. "Let's go tend the horses, then we'll eat something. I have some fried pies left, and maybe we can make hot coffee. I wish your father could eat, but guess it is better that he sleeps."

"I'll have to find some kindling wood, Preacher. We hain't had no fire all day. Guess we best have one now though. Pa shore don't need to chill."

After they had turned out the horses in the fenced enclosure and finished their sparse meal, John felt a lot better. He lay on a bearskin rug across from the dancing flames and listened to the whine of the wind. This place sure would scare the girls, he thought. Getting up, he checked on the old man again. He seemed to be breathing well and it looked like he was sleeping normally. John offered up another silent prayer, then placed the blanket close around Mr. Price. Settling down again on his pallet, he was soon asleep in the soothing warmth of the fire.

John did not know how long he had been asleep when he was awakened by someone yelling and banging on the door.

"We'uns want ter see Burl," someone shouted. "Open up in thar a'fore we break the door in!"

John heard Tad remove the plank bar and felt the rush of cold air hit his face as he sat up. The grumble of voices outside became clearer.

"Wal, if'n Burl hain't home, whar's yer old man? Go git old Price. He kin sell likker I reckon."

John heard Tad trying to explain that his father was laid up. Then the door was thrown open violently, and the men stomped in. John rolled back against the old man's bunk to avoid being trampled on.

"Whar is he?" a harsh voice asked. "Yer old man kin take keer of us jest as good as Burl." As Tad lit the lamp, John looked at the tough faces, all scrubby with beards, under the black hats. Each man cradled a rifle in his arm. One seemed to be in charge of the others.

"Whar's yer old man, Tad?" he asked. Then he paused when he saw the bunk. John looked around too, he saw that Price was awake and glaring at the man with intense hatred.

"Pa be sick," Tad began again, his face white with fear. "This here be the preacher from down below. I done fetched him to help fix Pa up." He turned to John.

John stood up and held out his hand. "I'm John Nilson," he said, "from the church down in the valley toward Gentry."

"Wal, I be gawdamned!" the leader swore, spitting at John's feet. "Never thought I'd see the day old Price'd take up with a preacher!" The three men roared with laughter. Turning to the old man he added, "Price, we'uns come fer likker. Now tell this here young'un of yours jest whar hit be, so we can git the hell out a'fore sunup."

When the old man did not answer, the ruffian gave the bunk a hard kick, swore, and aimed his rifle at Tad.

"Now, kid, if'n ye got a lick of sense, ye'll fetch us some lightening right fast."

"Yeah, we ain't got all night," another man agreed.

In alarm John stepped in front of Tad and explained to them again. "Mr. Price is not able to talk or move. We don't know what the matter is. We may have to get him down the mountain to help. It would be well if all of you left and came back again later." John felt helpless in view of their rifles, but knew he had to make a stand.

"Wal, if'n the old coot cain't move, guess we best help ourselves." The leader moved swiftly to the back of the cabin. John saw him disappear, then come back to get the lamp and signal for the other two to follow. To John's surprise they vanished behind a quilt hanging on the wall. He saw that there was an opening behind it, and knew it must lead to a tunnel or dug-out. Tad got up and hurriedly followed the men, leaving John alone with Old Man Price. John took his hand and felt him struggle. He was trying to speak.

"Don't be alarmed, Mr. Price," John warned, trying to quiet him. "Just let them alone and they will leave as soon as they find what they want." The old man began to moan and John felt him move. Then he felt the cold barrel of a rifle and knew Price had found his gun. Wishing desperately for a light, John felt around for wood to feed the fire. His nerves could not stand much more of this darkness. Finding a few chips, he threw them on the coals.

As the flames flickered up, John saw the figure on the bunk with the rifle aimed at the quilt on the wall. Before he could decide what he should do, the quilt moved and Tad emerged. Close behind were the three men with the leader carrying the lamp. They did not have any jugs so John knew they had not found Price's whiskey. Before a word could be said the rifle exploded and the ruffian behind Tad fell. The next man immediately fired at Price, but was a second too slow. Price had swung his rifle and fired again. The ruffian's bullet splintered the log inches from John's head, as Price's bullet had deflected his aim. With a grotesque look of surprise, he fell across the still body of the first man. The ruffian leader gave a wild yell and made for the door, just as Tad caught the lamp. Before Price could aim, the terrified man made it out into the darkness, and stumbled down the incline to the horses. Soon they heard a horse crashing up the trail that led to Missouri.

John felt like he was in a dream. Then, realizing the enormity of what had taken place, he got to his feet and walked over to the two fallen men to check for a pulse. Tad came over and took hold of his arm.

"Tain't no use feeling of them fellers, Preacher. When my pa shoots at ye, they's jest no chance fer man ner beast. Bet Pa done got most of them that has tried to do him wrong. Most don't even try. Tonight they jest thought he was helpless," Tad spoke with pride.

Glancing at the bunk John saw that the old man was quiet and watching them intently.

"What will we do now, Tad?" John asked. "We should call the coroner. Do you know who these men are and where they might have come from?"

"Cain't be sure, but reckon they be friends of Burl's, come after likker. Guess they didn't know Burl be gone. Don't know their names, but Pa may know. He sure did come to in a hurry. Wish he'd tell me what to do now. Guess you and me will have to dig a hole and git rid of these polecats." Tad looked contemptuously at the two bodies.

"We can't do that Tad," John objected. "We must get word to the authorities. But we can get them outside, away from your father. One of us will have to ride to Gentry in the morning."

At this remark the old man groaned and sat up. Pointing to a wooden box beside the hearth he signaled Tad to look in it. Tad reached in and found a jug. He hurried over with it to his father. Taking a long drink, Old Man Price shuddered violently. Then, wiping his dripping beard on his sleeve, he turned on John.

"We'uns will take keer of them skunks," he told John, looking at the men laying on the dirt floor. "I ain't dead yet, Preacher. Tad hadn't ought to have fetched ye. But seeing as how hit be done, ye will jest hep him dig a hole and come sunrise, we'll git rid of them varmints. Think they can git the best of a Price, do they!" He groaned again and lay back on the bunk.

"Pa, I done the only thing I knowed," Tad defended himself. "Shore had to do something. Ye said that old Granny had hexed ye, and we both heered that the preacher warn't a'feared of her. He must hev hepped ye too."

"Wal, hain't saying he did and hain't saying he didn't, but my own corn hepped me the most. Now drag them two polecats out the door till morning. Maybe the wolves can save us the burying," the old man laughed. "Now bar thet door and shet that lamp off," he ordered as he closed his eyes.

John had trouble getting to sleep again. Reviewing the events of the night, he thought that he must have been dreaming. The girls would never believe him this time. He was worried too about not calling the authorities. He knew he would have to make a report when he got down the mountain. Could the old woman really have put a spell on Mr. Price? Something had happened to him. His thoughts went around in circles until weariness took over at last and he slept.

The next morning John helped Tad dig a grave below the cabin and they slid the two men, wrapped in old ragged quilts, into it, Then they placed rocks on the mound to discourage the wolves from digging them up.

"If'n their kin want to come dig 'em up, they will be able to find the place," Tad said. "Bet that there one thet got away don't never show his face around here again. Not many people fool with Pa and live to tell hit."

The note of pride in the boy's voice grated on John's nerves. "Tad, you know it's wrong to kill. That is one of the Ten Commandments in the Bible."

"All I got ter say is, God never lived up here on Sawtooth," Tad replied. "If'n God keered so much about we'uns, why did he let my Ma die off and leave us?"

"It is not God's fault that bad things happen," John hastened to explain. "Man brings most of his troubles on himself by living in the wrong way. Do you believe it is right for your father to be making whiskey? If it hadn't been for the whiskey those men wouldn't have come up here in the first place."

"I guess that's so," Tad said grudgingly. "But Pa's likker is a sight better than that poison stuff that can kill a man off."

John made no answer. The boy was right and they both knew it. When people wanted whiskey they would buy it somewhere, no matter how rotten it was. Going back into the cabin he saw Price was awake.

"I be powerful hongry, Tad," he complained. "Fire up them coals and make me some coffee and cornpone." Then he looked hard at John and pointed. "Now I'm telling ye, Preacher, this here is nobody's business but ourn. Ye jest go on down off this mountain and keep your mouth shet. Jest say I be better. I don't want no lawman snooping around this mountain, and ye better jest do as I tell ye. Never held with no preachers much, but ye was real neighborly to ride up just to do we'uns a kindness. So if'n ever ye need our help, jest send the word."

Before John could think of an answer the old man went on. "Me and Tad make out right good mostly. Cain't say what come over me, but I blame hit on that old Granny. She be powerful mad when I run her off. She is the devil's womern and I don't hold with none of her ways. Poor folks up above here shore be in fer it. Hope they run her clean to Missouri. Hope they ain't a'feared to cross her." He sank back exhausted.

John wanted to object and say he intended to report the incident, but decided against it. Anxious to head home, he held out his hand to the old man.

"I am glad to see you feeling better, Mr. Price," he told him. "I can't condone what's been done here this morning, but I know how strongly you feel. If you and Tad have any more trouble and need me, I'll come back. I would also like to invite you both to our church service." John knew the old man wasn't likely to accept.

"I use ter go when I was a boy. My pappy lived in Tennessee and we'uns all went to church. He raised tobacco and corn too," the old man chuckled. "Me and ma would of taken our boys to meeting here but there be none then. Now it's jest too late. Tad is welcome to go if'n he is so minded to. I'd best stay and watch out fer more of them polecats. Mark my word, they will be more. If'n ye hear old faithful booming don't git skeered," he said as he patted his rifle with his bony hand.

"Well, if you change your mind you are always welcome," John offered again. "If I can ever be of any help, just let me know. I want to go now. I believe you will be alright with Tad's help."

"We'll be fine, Preacher, s'long as that old womern don't show up again," Tad told him. Together they went out and caught John's mare. It was with relief that John started back down the trail.

As he rode, John thought that this kind of thing did not happen in modern times. Yet he knew these hills were in a backwash of time. As he took the trail that led down to the church, he could see the wisp of smoke from the chimney at home. Already the sun was about to disappear behind the mountain. Turning the mare loose, he forked down some hay for her, and gave her a pat. She needed rest, as he intended to ride to Gentry the next day and do his duty. Going in the back door John called, "Anybody here that will feed a hungry man?"

Ann and Kate both came running to the kitchen. "Wal, did ye decide ter come home?" Katie asked. "What did ye find on up to Prices'?"

Slowly, with his arm around Ann, John disbelievingly told them all about the shooting and the burying of the two men.

"I intend to ride into Gentry tomorrow to inform the authorities," he concluded.

"Ye'd best let well enough alone," Katie warned. "Thet there hain't the first hole dug on old man Price's mountain. If'n they tried to find them all, hit shore would take a mite of time."

"You may be right, Kate," John agreed, "but I feel I have to do what is right."

"Ye'll jest stir up trouble if'n ye do and ye might jest set old Granny on us agin. She ain't one ter fool with," Kate said.

"Oh John, do you have to go? Maybe Katie knows best," Ann said. She was alarmed by the events up on Sawtooth and did not want any more trouble with Granny. God knew she had caused enough as it was.

John knew when he was outnumbered, but while lying awake that night, he knew he had to do it. The next day he told them he had calls to make, then he detoured back around and headed for the store. He waited until he could get Yancey alone, then explained what had happened.

"I feel I should notify someone about the deaths," he told the big man.

"You do what you think is best," Yancey warned, "but in these hills it sometimes pays not to see or hear too much." John caught the finality in his voice.

"But how could I not see," John protested, "when I had to help dig their grave?"

"I know how you must feel," Yancey agreed. "All right, I'll put in the call to Siloam. They don't have a deputy any closer." He turned the crank on the old phone.

While he reported the incident to the sheriff's office, John felt a reluctance on the part of the man taking down the information. He was told that if they could spare a man, someone might be up in a day or so. When John reported the conversation to Yancey, he saw a smile on the Irishman's face.

"This county don't want any part of the hill feuds," he told John. "If anyone comes at all, it will be a federal man and he'll be looking for Price's still."

"I can not believe they would overlook a killing like this," John protested.

"Hill people are always fighting," Yancey explained gently. "You said yourself that those men were armed. Price was only protecting his own life and property. They couldn't put him in jail for that. Just for making whiskey."

John saw his point and had to agree. Still, he had done what he thought was right and could live with his conscious. Yancey warned him again to keep quiet.

"Best to let things lay, John," he repeated. "After you have lived among these people as long as I have, you will know that I'm right."

The ride home seemed to take longer than usual. It was clear he didn't understand the reasoning of the natives. He thought he had enough to worry about without Mr. Price too. He sensed Ann had changed in the past few weeks. She seemed to act like she enjoyed life here. He knew time was a healer, but he was still puzzled at times. One day she seemed so happy, then the next she was nervous and worried. I won't tell the girls that I called, he decided.

John did not hear anything from Sawtooth, and none of the hill people mentioned the Prices or the mill. In fact, for several days John felt it was too quiet. He could sense people knew all about the matter and were being close-mouthed. He finally relaxed enough to help Bud plant his corn on a slope behind the cabin. John could not help but thinking that a hard rain would wash the seeds away; yet, he knew that Bud had had a good stand the previous fall. The girls were busy cooking, and expected Tom to come home any day. John was concerned for Ann: she had been feeling bad for several days, and had very little appetite. With these fresh worries, the grave on Sawtooth gradually faded from his mind.

⊰ Chapter Seventeen ⊱

Ann's chores seemed to multiply in the warm, spring days. Her small flock of hens were setting, her garden sprouted weeds overnight, and she had spring cleaning to do. Katie agreed to help her. While they were busy, Katie told Ann she must be in the family way. Alarmed, Ann thought of her day with Bill. It would be her just reward, but it would hurt John. She loved him more than she had ever loved Bill. She begged Katie not to tell John until she was sure, but in her heart she knew she was going to be a mother. Oh God, let it be John's baby she thought.

She remembered the night right after Bill had made love to her. John had seemed to need her love with a renewed hunger and Ann had been surprised at his intensity that night. Maybe that had been the night. Silently she prayed it was.

Finally the secret came out, and John was alarmed at how weak she was feeling. He tried to get her to go to Siloam for a checkup. Ann told him it was only her condition and Katie agreed, saying most women got sick every morning.

"Miss Ann looks right pert to me," she told John. "Even if'n she does get to feeling poorly, we'uns can go get Hattie."

"We'll wait, we'll wait," John agreed, still doubting the wisdom of it.

When Ann got up and left in the middle of the Sunday service, she saw amused glances and knew the women had guessed her condition. She wondered what they would think if they knew she was worried about who the father was. They would think less of her than Kate. God, she prayed, let this baby have blue eyes.

Katie and Ann went fishing on Burnt Creek the day Tom came home. Ann wanted some trout, and had persuaded Katie to go with her. Katie baited all of the hooks using earthworms, a job Ann detested. They soon had their basket full of the gleaming fish so they headed back to the cabin.

"Now all we'uns need is some cornpone and fried taters," Katie said.

"Oh yes, with some hot coffee and berry pie afterward," Ann agreed. "I sure wish we had a fresh lemon."

"Tain't no use wishing cause they ain't none around here," Kate answered. "We'uns got good vinegar and I'll make up some dressing fer them fish thet will taste jest as good."

As they passed the path where she had made love to Bill, Ann's heart beat harder. She glanced at Kate, afraid she could read her thoughts. She was almost afraid she would hear Granny's laugh again. Making her nerves be still, she managed to get on out to the road. Katie saw him first.

"He's coming! Tom's coming!" And she started to run down the trail.

Shading her eyes Ann saw a distant figure with a suitcase. She knew it was Tom and that he had walked all of the way from the store. She sat down to rest on a log so the two young people could have a few minutes to themselves. The air was heavy with the perfume of spring flowers and butterflies laced the breeze. Some chipmunks inspected Ann, decided she was harmless, and went chattering about their business. She could hear the gurgle of Burnt Creek behind her. This was a magic place, yet nature could be cruel. These people knew the seasons well, and had plenty of time to prepare for changes in the weather. Any who were too lazy to work had to suffer. Not many of the families were that shiftless, except the Perkins. Will would never change, but soon Little Luke would be big enough to help his mother. Ann wondered about the child growing inside of her. She wanted a blonde, little son that looked like John. If this baby was dark, how could she know for sure whose child it was? Watching a milkweed wave in the wind, she thought about how fragile the little life was that she was carrying. Feeling so uncertain about every part of her life, she got up and walked out to meet Tom and Kate.

"Well now, how's my new patient?" Tom asked happily. "Kate says that you are very excited."

"I'm glad to see you, Tom," Ann said. "John was trying to get me to Siloam. He doesn't know that it is natural for me to feel bad the first few weeks."

"Do you know about when to expect this little fellow?" Tom asked. "You know I have to go back for summer classes, but I'll have a few days in early September."

"I don't know," Ann answered with fear in her heart.

"Now don't ye fret," Katie soothed. "I bet Hattie will take keer of you and come and stay the last few days if ye ask her."

"John wouldn't like that," Ann objected. "and its not that he doesn't think a lot of Hattie. He will still insist that I go to Siloam to a hospital."

"Well now, Miss Ann, don't worry yet," Tom begged. "We'll see how you do the rest of this summer, and I may just get back for the big event. Katie would want to be here I know." Tom knew he had to spend all of his time during the summer in classes if he was going to earn his diploma and come back here where he was so desperately needed. He also wanted to line up some part-time work, and to find a place for him and Katie to live. Walking on to the parsonage, the three caught up with all of the news.

"Doc Goshorn says I take to medicine like a fish to water," Tom said proudly. "He has been letting me go with him on calls. I've already caught up with the two years of study at Siloam."

"Hain't he smart?" Katie beamed. "I shore hope I can be of some help to him later on when he goes calling on folks."

"I am sure Hattie can teach you a lot of stuff now, Katie." Ann told her.

"You know, when I get through I'll be able to operate," Tom stated with awe. "I wish Ma could have lived to see it. She always said that reading so many books was just wasting my time."

"I know your mother would have been proud to know that you are going to be a doctor," Ann comforted him. "And who knows, perhaps she can see you from where she is now."

"Ye mean she be watching us from up there, Miss Ann?" Kate asked fearfully.

"I don't really know for sure, Katie, but my Aunt Cora in Denver attends meetings where they talk of this. Many people believe that only your body changes and your spirit is free then."

"Don't be afraid, Katie," Tom told her, holding her little body close, and her long hair tangled against his shoulder. "If Ma can see what we are doing, she will be proud of both of us."

When they came to the clearing around the cabin, the door opened and John walked out. He eagerly crossed the porch and took Tom's hand in his.

"You are a welcome sight, Tom," he told the young man. "This wife of yours has worn us out asking what day it is, and wanting to go to Gentry in hopes of meeting you there." John's blue eyes twinkled as he saw Kate flush with embarrassment.

"Guess I be a mite anxious," Katie admitted, her dark eyes lowered, "but I been jest that lonesome, Tom. Not that I hain't been fine here with the Preacher and Miss Ann."

"It's alright, Katie," Ann told her. "I'd be lonesome too if John ever went off for more than a day or two."

It was pure enjoyment to sit out on the porch that evening and listen to the katydids sing. Even the bullfrogs down on Burnt Creek carried on their concert in a spirited manner. Tom and John talked about the needs in the hills for them both to fill. John would heal their spirits and Tom their bodies. When the mournful howl of a wolf drifted down from Sawtooth, John thought of his night at the Prices' and told Tom about it. Watching the pattern made by the waving pine branches in the moonlight, Ann was glad to be here with those she loved.

"That could bring the federal men down on Mr. Price," the young man said. "It might have been better not to have reported it. I know how you feel, Preacher, but you don't understand how it is here in these hills. People just don't tell on each other. It is kinda like a code of honor. I doubt Yancey will spread it around though."

Ann looked at Tom in surprise, and saw that John was too. She knew John had made a mistake. Seeing Katie and Tom sitting close in love, she moved her chair over by John.

It seemed to Ann that the summer raced away. As each golden day blended into memory, she could not think of a time when she had felt so happy. She and Katie visited around with John. Usually there was some need to be met. If a mother was sick, they helped clean, cook, and even wash clothes. She saw that most of the children were without summer underwear or shoes. She wished she could start a used clothing store. Aunt Cora had responded once, but with all the wrong things—these people did not need silks, satins, or high-heeled shoes. Her days were happy as she did her bit to help. Only when Bill's angry face intruded, and she could hear old Granny's laugh, did her mind walk in worried circles again.

Tom was able to use his new medical knowledge during the week he was home. When Effie's and Bud's little Mary came over with a bad toothache, Tom used his slender pliers to pull the tooth. He had clean cotton to swab it with and an aspirin powder that he used to fill the hole. The Childers looked at him with awe. He also made a trip to the Perkins' place when Luke took sick. Luke seemed to be all eyes as he lay in the big bed in the front room. His cheeks were sunken and his blonde hair stuck out in all directions like straw. Ann had thought he just didn't get enough to eat, but Tom said it was stomach fever and worms. The girls took him cookies and cold cider. All too soon Tom had to leave for summer school.

About mid-summer John took both girls with him one morning early to see how Lucy and Eli were getting along. The old man had been up for a few weeks but still was not able to ride his mule to town. Kate was afraid, but Ann and John talked her into going. They found Eli sitting by the big, black kitchen stove in Lucy's deep rocker. His face looked thin and gaunt, and his hair was straggling over his collar. There was no welcome in his eyes when they came in behind Lucy.

"Pa, ye got company," the beaming little woman told him. "Katie and the Preacher and his wife be here."

"Hain't no company of mine," the old man grumbled, then sat forward and looked hard at John. In a shaky voice he asked, "I heered tell that Old Man Price hain't been doing no good here lately?"

"Yes, Mr. Price has been sick," John said guardedly.

"I heered tell that he had a mite of trouble too," he prodded.

"I'm afraid he did," John admitted in an attempt to cut the matter off.

"Hit don't make no mind," Eli sighed, sinking back in the

rocker. "I know what went on. Ye don't hev to tell me a thang. Old Granny shore will git him yet. Hit jest don't pay to cross her, I know."

"Now, Pa, don't ye fault yerself so. We'uns will do jest fine now thet old womern be gone." Lucy was busy getting them all seated. "Katie, how be Tom at that big, fine school?"

"He be just fine, Ma. I wish he could be here now. I bet he could hep Pa right now," Kate said.

"I don't know, Katie," John objected. "But I do think he should get up and try to walk around some, and not just sit in this chair so much. He ought to get out in the sunshine more."

"Thet be jest what I been telling him," Lucy agreed. "He hain't going to git no better jest a'setting and rocking all day long. Now you folks jest set still a spell and we'uns will eat some spiced peaches and cream." Lucy was like a mother hen, so happy to have company to talk to. She placed a loaf of home-made bread and a pitcher of thick cream on the oilcloth covered table. Pulling Eli's chair up to the table, she gave him a bowl. The old man sat as if asleep and did not touch it. Occasionally he would look up and stare for a long moment. His piercing eyes gave Ann the creeps, but she felt obliged to offer help.

"Lucy, let me help Eli. These peaches are so good. I know he would enjoy some."

Struggling to sit erect, Eli spoke. "Ye best stay from Sawtooth." Then turning toward John, he added. "Ye think she be gone but she be still close by. I hain't got no use for the lot of ye, but I done my rightful duty and ye be warned. Now ye pay heed ter what I say." Once again he repeated the warning, "Stay away from Sawtooth Mountain!"

Ann looked at Eli with alarm, but he had sank back in the chair with his eyes closed. Surely he was just a senile old man and they did not need to worry about what he had said. Then she saw John's face. If he was beginning to worry, she could not help but worry too. Soon the talk turned to Lucy and how she was getting along here doing all of the work.

"Mrs. Tate, I would be happy to come over and help out," John promised. "I could dig your potatoes and onions, and anything else you need done. How about your corn? Will there be enough to last you through the winter?"

"I shore could use a little hep with the digging, but ye have enough to do going around and calling on everybody," she said.

"Now, Lucy," Ann objected. "I want John to help you. Katie can come too."

"I shore would be beholden to ye, John, if'n ye and Kate could come. That old sow already been rooting them sweet taters. I jest cain't seem to fix that pen to keep her in. Be glad when she be lard and sausage." Then looking over at the old man slumped in his chair, she added, "Pa here cain't hep me none."

"Then it is settled," John said. "Katie will come and you both can have a good visit."

When they left, old Eli sat as before, his eyes looking far off in the distance, and he did not seem aware that they were gone.

Katie and John kept up a lively conversation as they bumped along on the spring seat of the wagon. They could not believe the change in Eli and Lucy. She seemed to be so happy to finally be the boss of her life. Ann's thoughts went around in circles, wondering where Granny was right now. as she eased her back against an old comforter, she saw that her waist was slowly filling out. The tiny life inside was growing. Looking up at the lazy summer clouds, she saw a black hawk slowly circling the tall pines. Shaking her fist at the hawk, she vowed she would beat this and make John happy yet in spite of the old hag!

⌁ Chapter Eighteen ⌁

Two or three weeks after Eli's dire warning. John returned with Kate and caught up Lucy's chores. Katie told Ann how wonderful it had been to be at home all day with her mother. They had talked, and looked through all of the keepsakes in one of Lucy's old trunks. Among the treasures was an old gizzard patch quilt, yellow with age, that had been her grandmother's. Most of the pieces were homespun, made by the old lady over a century ago. Katie reported that Eli had slept most of the time, but he had sat out on the porch for awhile. He had muttered at John while he worked in Lucy's garden.

Ann had begun to feel restricted, because John would not let her wander off to the creek anymore. She was delighted when she heard that there was to be a pie social at the schoolhouse in Gentry. She and Katie worked all day on Friday making their pies. She had learned a lot about baking since moving into the parsonage. She often wondered what her aunt would say about their primitive kitchen. Looking at her hands she remembered what Bill had said. Well, she could not play lady here, but sometimes she longed for the comforts she had left behind.

The school grounds were alive with people when they got there. Ann was surprised at the large crowd. Long tables were spread in the school yard out under big oak trees. Men were taking turns at the big, wooden ice cream freezers that were sitting in tubs of ice. Yancey kept them supplied with blocks of ice from his storehouse. Ann was surprised to see how thick they still were, even now after summer was half gone. There would be ice left even after the river froze again. Thick dust rose on the playground where some boys were playing ball. Some of the little girls were swinging, and Ann saw the Perkins girls among them.

Ann and Kate walked over and took a seat at one of the tables, spread with a sheet made of bleached-out white flour sacks. John was soon deep in talk with the hill men. Ann was content to watch the crowd and wait for the treat to come. She saw several curious glances her way, and was surprised at Kate's giggle.

"They be making guesses about when yore young'un will be getting here," Kate told her. "Jest look at that Lettie May. She be making eyes at every boy she sees," she said.

"I hate to think of her getting married so soon," Ann said. "She better have fun now."

"She shore hain't as lucky as I be," Katie agreed. "My Tom be the pick of these hills."

The crowd soon settled down as the wonderful treats were dished up. Ann tasted the wonders: creamy peach, strawberry, chocolate, and vanilla ice cream; and pies of all varieties. Ann saw one of Hattie's angel cakes and wondered just how she could make it rise so high.

"Jest be sure there be thirteen whites of eggs from domineker hens," was the way Hattie explained her secret, "and mix them up with a wood fork." Hattie beamed proudly around the serving table, as the people passed by filling their plates with the good things.

Ann thought they would have to go home soon as it was nearing dusk. Then she saw some men building a bonfire against the mountain chill. One time her heart lurched as she caught a glimpse of a tall, dark man who resembled Bill. Feeling faint, she suddenly sat down suddenly by the side of a startled hill woman she did not know. Katie and John rushed over to see if she was alright. Gaining her composure, she smiled and told them she guessed she had just eaten too much. She was thinking how awful it would be if Bill did come back and John found out the whole sorry story. Kate told her they were not ready to go home yet.

"We'uns may be going to have story telling," said Kate. "Ye never heered sich tales like can be told in these hills after dark!" The simple girl shivered in anticipation.

"What kind of stories?" asked Ann.

"Probably ghost stories and spirits. There be lots of strange things go on. Ma used to laugh and Pa would get fighting mad. He said someday the old devil would meet up with her, and then she would larn a thing or two."

Ann and John laughed, and said they didn't believe either. But Ann knew witches were real. Everyone was afraid of Granny, and she had strange powers. Soon, the first man, a stranger, got up to talk.

He told the crowd that one night he was alone in his cabin near the Missouri line while his family was visiting relatives a few miles away helping take care of a mother and new baby. During the night, he awoke and heard the handle turning on his porch cistern. It was pitch dark. He heard the back door bolt slide back, followed by the sound of heavy footsteps on the kitchen floor. Next, he heard the bucket of water plop on the table, and some spill out on the floor. Then the dipper rattled, as if someone was getting a drink. The old man said he jumped up, lit his lamp, and rushed into the kitchen, but found no one there. The back door was still bolted on the inside, the bucket of water was full on the table, and the floor was wet. He said he slept in the barn the rest of that night, and every night until his family returned.

The next speaker was Grandpa Holcomb, whom Ann had seen before hanging around Yancey's store. He said that when he was a young man he lived in a house that had been built many years before during the wars with the indians. While his elders sat in the kitchen by the stove, he was sent to bed with several smaller children. The room where his pallet was laid was almost dark. There was just enough light from the kitchen lamp to see objects. As he lay half asleep an indian clad only in a loin cloth and headband walked out of a small lean-to storeroom carrying a hatchet in his hand. He stood at the foot of the pallet and looked intently at him. Then the indian turned as if to go into the kitchen where his parents and relatives were sitting and talking. Grandpa Holcomb said that he screamed then as loud as he could, and the indian ran back into the lean-to. When his folks came they searched the room, the lean-to, the porch, and the yard, but did not find anyone. The old timers told them it must have been an indian chief who had been killed on that farm during a raid years before.

After that story Ann began to feel cold, so John went to their wagon for a blanket. Katie giggled and said she was just scared.

Another man got up, put a log on the fire, and told a tale about the Ghost of Paris, a story known all over the Ozarks. The ghost was a woman who always dressed in black and carried a cane. She usually haunted the town only during the fall and winter months. The story went that she had been jilted by her sweetheart, a confederate soldier, and that when she was dying, she swore to come back and haunt the lover who had since married another woman. Her former lover had moved away soon after that, and she was often seen wandering around. Many children had been frightened by her. The old man who told the story said he had once seen his uncle and cousins run clear down the main street, hollering that the haint was after them.

A chuckle went around the tables, but subdued as many people peered into the dark shadows around them. Ann wished that they could go home. She knew that it would take a good hour to make the five miles up the dark trail, and knew the old log parsonage would look good to her this night.

To her surprise, Bud Childers stood up near the fire and began to talk. Bud seemed to be very serious as he faced the crowd. He told them that he had seen a "booger dog" many times up above the mill. He said it was nearly as big as a cow, and was like a spotted hound. The first time he had seen it, he was so surprised that he almost fell off of his mule. As he went back to his place to sit down, several others claimed to have seen it too. Some said it was all white, and others claimed they had seen a black one. One man claimed he had thrown an ax at it, and it had gone right through and lodged in a tree. Others said they had shot at the strange creature and the bullet had passed right through tne dog.

Ann was particularly interested in a story about Sawtooth Mountain. She had heard about the noises that often frightened riders caught up there after dark. The trail ran straight up past Price's mill and around the other side, where it joined a larger road that led down to the Missouri line. It seemed that a cabin close by had been haunted for more than forty years. The old settlers who had lived there had killed a peddler to get his goods, and had buried his body under a lean-to shed. The peddler's ghost started groaning and knocking on the shed floor after a few days. This would commence each evening about dark. Finally the settlers left for parts unknown. Several hill families tried to live there since, but had finally given up. The lean-to had been torn down and a search was made for the peddler's bones. Nothing was ever found. The cabin still stands but everyone avoids it. People that are forced to ride that trail at night claim to hear smothered screams, as if someone is being tortured. One man, who was said to live near Little Rock, claimed that he had met the devil near the old cabin. He said he had shaken hands with him, and his hand had been burned up to his elbow. Several people around the fire nodded in agreement, and said that they had seen him with one hand gone.

By this time Ann was more than ready to leave. The night breeze and the darkness seemed to lend credence to the tall tales she had heard. She almost expected to see Granny's evil face in the shadows. John had been watching her and decided she had heard enough, so they slipped away to their wagon. Even the mare seemed to be spooked. She shied at every noise along the trail. By the time they reached home, they all agreed that most of the stories had been exaggerated. But Kate insisted that there was some truth in them. She said she had heard all of the tales at family gatherings and added that Eli had seen the "booger dog" too. He had seen it in the bottom land where he always planted his sweet potatoes. Their old hound, Molly, must have seen it too, because she ran for home and would not come out from under their cabin for several days.

"At any rate," Katie stated nervously, "this kind of a night makes a body scairy. Ma used ter say hit war as black as midnight under a skillet. That shore would be right ternight. Best we'uns git a fire started. I shore be gitting the trembles."

Laughing bravely the three stomped in by way of the back porch. John made a fire in the fireplace and then went out to put up the mare. Ann thought about the stories they had heard and found it hard to sleep. It irked her to hear John's even breathing. The evening's events did not seem to disturb him at all. Of course he did not have a guilty conscious to worry him like she did. She wished at that moment that she was free again and not pregnant. It was then she felt the little life inside her move for the first time. Too late, too late, this child was coming. Please, let it have blue eyes, she thought. The night seemed to bring back Granny's laugh once again to Ann.

A few days later a letter came from Aunt Cora. It seemed that the venerable lady had serious doubts about a descendant of hers being born in the boondocks of the Ozarks. Ann couldn't suppress her laughter as she read the letter aloud to John. Her aunt demanded that she come home to Denver for an examination, and also said she must not let the natives touch her, especially a midwife.

"Your aunt doesn't think much of our good folks here," John observed thoughtfully, his blue eyes laughing. Then anxiously, "Ann, maybe you should see a doctor."

"Not in Denver," Ann objected. "Tom says there are some good doctors in Siloam Springs. I had thought of going there and being checked, but I feel perfectly well. So, why worry?"

So the matter rested. A nice letter was written to calm Aunt Cora, and Ann did not bring up the subject again. She hardly relished a wagon trip to Gentry now, and much less riding the mail truck into Siloam Springs. There was much consternation later in the month when John brought home Aunt Cora's reply. She, it seemed, did not trust either of them. She was going to pay them a visit and would arrive at Gentry sometime the following week.

"Oh John," Ann cried, "whatever shall we do?"

"Why, we will meet her and enjoy her visit," he answered. "It will be good for you to see your aunt. The three of you can visit, and you and Katie can take her calling on some of your friends. Why, she probably won't want to leave."

"You don't know my aunt very well," Ann disagreed. "This

place has to be really cleaned up. I've let too much go this summer. And I don't think it would be a good idea for her to do much visiting. She thinks we live in a heathen land as it is." Ann's troubled face made him hurt in his heart. Was she ashamed of how they lived?

"Katie will help you clean the cabin. Besides, this place is fine just as it is. As long as you are here in it, anyplace is wonderful to me," he said holding her close.

It was a busy week for all of them. Ann insisted on cleaning the cabin from top to bottom. She and Kate did up the curtains, and John took the braided rugs out to air in the sun. Kate had decided to go and stay a few days with her mother while Aunt Cora visited. Summer would be over soon and Kate was excited about leaving the hollow for "furrin parts". Now that Eli was not in a position to object, they could have a nice visit. It was decided that Ann would not go to meet her aunt at the store. John would pick her up in the wagon. As far as they knew, the mail truck would bring her on Friday afternoon.

Ann could visualize her aunt lecturing the driver about the holes and bumps along the dirt road from Siloam. The trip would take a long time because the driver would have to stop at all of the mail boxes along the way. The girls baked for hours on Thursday. John told them that one lady could never eat so much.

It was with a sense of foreboding that John left on Friday afternoon. About mid-afternoon, he pulled up to Yancey's store with a list of things to buy for Ann. He thought that by the time he had selected them, the mail truck would be in.

As he stepped up on the porch he thought the loafers sitting on their cane chairs were looking at him oddly. He wondered why nobody spoke. Entering the store he saw big Yancey behind the counter. The friendly man motioned him closer. "You have a visitor back there," he whispered. "She's been here over an hour and I think she may be just a little mad." Yancey's blue eyes twinkled, and John could see a slight smile cross his face.

John turned and there she was. He had a quick mental picture of Hattie's bantam hen with her feathers ruffled, ready to fight all comers. Aunt Cora was dressed for travel. Her white hair was tucked under a ruffled cap, and she was encased in a long cape, which was drawn carefully around her. Underneath it she wore a black alpaca, starched suit. John saw that she was dusty, and that the shine was gone from her black shoes. Beside her were several bags. One look from her piercing, blue eyes was enough for John. She was bristling because she had not been met right on the dot. John started marshalling his defenses, and wished to heaven he had Ann with him.

"Young man," she began, "do you know how long I have been sitting on this hard chair waiting? Where is my niece, and why weren't you here when I arrived? Didn't you receive my letter? It would be no wonder if all of the mail comes in that old relic of a car that I had to ride in to get here. I do hope Ann isn't sick." The portly woman stopped to gasp for breath.

"Ann is fine, Aunt Cora," John reassured her quickly. "I would have been here sooner, but we thought it would take the mail longer to make the run." John was desperately trying to think of anything he could say to turn off her anger. He didn't relish hearing this tirade all the way home.

"Your man probably would not have arrived here until dark," she said, "but I told him I did not intend to sit in that antiquated truck all day. He could just bring me straight here, and do his stopping on his way back. I never saw such an ignorant person in all my days. Do you know that we had to stop three times in sixteen miles to put water in that vehicle?"

John could just see poor Bill trying to keep the old truck on the road while dodging Aunt Cora's verbal darts. There probably were a lot of mad people along the road when they had to wait for their mail.

"And another thing," Aunt Cora continued, "just when is this child due? Ann has no business coming so far away from civilization to have this precious child."

"You can talk to Ann about all of that as soon as we get home," John answered evasively. "I need to pick up a few things, then we'll head up the trail. How about a nice cool drink while you are waiting?" Seeing the lady's red face, John felt alarm for her blood pressure.

"Well, it is nice to know you do have water in this forsaken place," the tired woman replied. Yancey came over with a glass.

John gave his list to the big Irishman and saw the amusement in his eyes as he starting filling the order.

"Put in some tea," John requested. He remembered that Ann had said that her aunt did not drink coffee.

The trip back up the trail was trying for both of them. It seemed that the mare found every chuck hole on purpose. He felt at first that he should hurry, but when the old lady almost bounced off the high, spring seat, he slowed the mare down.

"Why in the world do you use this antique vehicle?" she wanted to know. "It seems to me that a car would be so much better, or even a good truck."

"A car could not make it over these trails," John explained patiently. "This road is poor, but most of them are much worse." He looked down at the grim face of his passenger. "You see, Aunt Cora, my people live all around these hills, and some places you cannot even use the wagon. I often have to ride my mare."

"I hope to heaven you are not letting Ann ride on this mangy beast," the old lady objected.

"No, not now," John hastened to say. "She has ridden though many times. Women here learn to ride early."

"Why in the world you gave up a good offer in a civilized

place to stay here in the backwoods, I will never know," the lady complained. "Ann could have a much easier life in Denver at that nice little church in the suburbs that I wrote her about."

With a start John realized that Ann had not told him about any offer for another church. She had stayed here of her own free will. Surely she did love him, and had forgotten the other man back in Denver. During the rest of the jolting ride home, he saw only the beauty of the hills, and the querulous voice of Aunt Cora did not bother him at all. The glow lasted right up to the kitchen door, where he stopped to assist her out of the wagon.

"Oh Ann," he called, "we are here. Your aunt is home." He wondered why she was not out to meet them.

"Do you mean to tell me," the old lady exclaimed, seeing the cistern, "that you draw water from a well? Ann did not tell me that your home was this primitive."

"Yes, we do," John told her. "It is the coldest, sweetest water that you will ever taste."

"Really," Aunt Cora answered suspiciously, eyeing John up and down. "Well, where is my niece?"

Holding open the back door, John wondered too. He drew out a chair for the tired woman and then made a quick check of the cabin. Ann was not there.

"She must have decided to take a little walk," he explained. He did not tell Cora that he had forbidden her to do this. "How about a cool drink or a cup of tea?" John invited her.

"I'll try your cold water," she agreed. "Then just show me to my room so I can wash this dust off. After that horrible ride I feel all shaken up."

With relief John went out to draw a fresh bucket of water. He hoped she would get over being mad before Ann returned. She surely would not have gone very far. After getting Aunt Cora settled in Katie's room, he took the mare to the shed and put up the wagon. Watching the path from the creek he finally saw Ann emerge from the trees. He hurried out to meet her.

"Ann, your aunt is here and is resting. I guess I had better warn you. She doesn't think much of me, the wagon, our roads, or the parsonage." Seeing Ann's look of dismay, he wished he had kept quiet.

"I didn't think she would," Ann smiled. "In fact, if we had a mansion it would be the same. The poor dear can always find something wrong. You must learn not to let it bother you. It is just her way. She is really a dear, though, and doesn't mean half of what she may say. Remember all of the things she has done to help us here. But I do worry that she may hurt Hattie's feelings, or some of the other women around here. She can say things so hard at times."

"Maybe you had better warn Hattie and tell her your aunt is a little peculiar," John laughed. He knew that would cover a multitude of faults. People could be excused for so many short-comings if they were labeled peculiar. He had felt that some of the hill people had even felt that way about him at times. Katie had intimated as much after the Christmas party.

"Now that is a terrible thing for the preacher to say," Ann teased. "We'll get by, but I do hope she doesn't hear any tales of witchcraft while she is here. That would be the last straw for my aunt." Also she was thinking that she hoped her aunt would not bring up the subject of Bill. She had better post Katie not to mention his visit. She wondered if John had heard. As if in answer the new life made its presence known. The next few days would be hard she knew.

⌁ Chapter Nineteen ⌁

During the first few days of Aunt Cora's visit, Ann caught up on the news of her friends in Denver. It sounded strange to her now: the accounts of parties, teas, charity drives, and showers. If she had not lost her head over a handsome, blonde preacher she would have been part of that scene. Now she was a dowdy, pregnant housewife. She wondered if she would ever be able to enjoy those kind of activities again. Thinking of the life and death problems here—Mr. Price, Eli Tate, and dear Katie—her life in Denver seemed like a dream from long ago. Feeling a surge of self-pity, she could not look at Aunt Cora for fear she would know how she felt. It would not take much for that dear lady to pack her up and insist on taking her back to Denver.

Almost a week went by before anyone came to call. This was the grace period allotted to everyone with company. She and John knew that the Sunday service would be well-attended because everyone would be curious about Aunt Cora. On Saturday morning Ann saw a wagon approaching in a cloud of dust from the Sawtooth trail. When it came closer she saw that it was Hattie and Jess Wilks and she gave a sigh of relief.

"Aunt Cora," she began, "here come two of our best friends. Hattie takes care of sick folks and is like a nurse to these people."

"Well thank goodness," the old lady snorted. "They need someone. If a person became very ill here, they would be in dire peril. One could die before a doctor could get up here over these cow trails. That is why you must come home and stay with me until this poor child is born." Aunt Cora was filled with righteous indignation. "Just look at yourself, child. You look as run down as some of the domestics I have had working for me."

Ignoring the remarks, Ann went to the door to welcome the visitors. Curiosity was evident on both sides, as they looked each other over.

"Hi, Miss Ann," Hattie greeted her. "This here must be yer relation come clear from the big city." She gazed admiringly at Aunt Cora.

"Oh yes, Hattie and Jess, do come in and meet my aunt," and Ann smiled in relief. "Aunt Cora, these are our dearest friends up here, the Wilks. Jess has a farm about five miles up the hollow."

"I hear you are a midwife and nurse to these people," the old lady stated with her usual bluntness.

"Yep," Jess answered with obvious pride. "Hattie here has been hepping sick folks since she was a slip of a girl. Some be born to hit ye know."

Aunt Cora did not comment on this bit of news and Ann hastily asked them to have coffee and pie. She knew there was always safety in eating and wished silently that Katie was there. Soon Hattie and Aunt Cora were busy talking about their favorite pie fillings.

"Did ye ever taste sweet tater pie?" Hattie questioned. "We'uns around here shore favor hit."

Aunt Cora had to admit that she had not had that pleasure.

She countered by asking, "Have you ever made my specialty of pineapple cream?"

Hattie had to confess that she had never even tasted pineapple. Ann was amazed to think that this could be possible, and told herself she would order some the next time she went to Yancey's store.

Before they had visited very long John came in from his trip up in the hills. Hattie asked him how Tom was making out at the big school. It was nice to tell her in front of Aunt Cora that some day they would have a doctor.

"We'uns know he shore will make a good'un," Jess added.

"Hit will be a pleasure fer me to hep Tom here," Hattie said.

"It will be nice to have a fine woman like you, Hattie, to help our doctor. I hope Katie can take some classes in First Aid this fall also," John said.

"She should learn about hygiene and nutrition, as well as first aid. She must prepare to be a doctor's wife."

"I think that is an excellent idea," Ann agreed, bridging the embarrassing silence. "I'm sure Katie will want to do anything to help Tom here."

So on a conciliatory note the Wilks left with Hattie looking guardedly but admiringly at the grand figure of Aunt Cora.

"She shore is a right smart lady," Hattie whispered to Ann as she climbed into the wagon.

"I hope she didn't hurt your feelings, Hattie," Ann said apologetically.

"Don't ye fret none over Hattie," Jess grinned. "She hain't got ary hurting bone in her." Jess slapped his leg over what to him was a funny subject.

"Bring yer aunty over anytime," Hattie invited. "We'uns can make pies." Then with a hearty laugh, the mountain couple drove on up the trail. Ann tried not to smile as she turned back to the porch and found her aunt watching.

"I like your mountain woman," she told a surprised Ann.

"But I thought you did not approve of her, or what she does," Ann said.

"Approve! Approve! What is there for me to judge? People have to do the best they can with what they have to do with. In this wilderness they wouldn't know how to act if they did have a professional nurse and doctor. From your letters I gather that most of their medicine is herbs, castor oil, and perhaps even witchery and spells."

"I'm afraid you are right," Ann sighed. "John and I can't believe the things that have happened here. We just keep hoping that we will be safe from harm." Then fearing she had said too much, she changed the subject and started to get their supper. She knew this was not the time to reveal all she knew of witchcraft here.

The Sunday morning service was an event in the little log church. Practically every family around came dressed in their best clothes. Effie Childers wore her heirloom shawl that was made of lamb's wool and had been handed down for nearly a century. It had only been worn to weddings and funerals and especially on days much cooler than this one. Jennie Perkin's hair, which was usually in disarray, was piled neatly on top of her head. Little Luke still wore poorly-patched overalls but had a jacket on which was unusual. Hattie as always looked neat and clean and so did her daughter Lettie May. Most of the men wore their black wide-brimmed hats, dark coats, and overalls. Few, like Bud, owned a good pair of dark pants.

Since coming to the hills Ann had put away her best dresses and worn simple cotton ones. However, with Aunt Cora here, she had decided that she should dress up for this service. Katie had helped let the seams out on one of her better skirts. She noted the admiring glances as they sat in their pew, and was amused to think that her out of style clothes would have made little impression in Denver. To these hill women they seemed very grand, especially Aunt Cora, in her velvet hat with a white ostrich feather. Aunt Cora's black broadcloth suit, with its starched tucked blouse made her an elegant figure. Even John must have felt Cora's influence. He had carefully brushed the good suit he usually reserved for funerals and weddings and was wearing it today.

It was after the service when people were standing in groups exchanging the week's news and also meeting Aunt Cora, that Ann heard a whisper of what was going on outside.

"I heered tell thet Leon Holcomb war in Yancey's store when the call came through. It war something about the killings up at the mill. They say the federal men air coming shore to snoop around." Ann was not sure who had whispered this bit of gossip in the group behind her, but the chuckle that followed identified the speaker as one on the Jones clan.

"Thet thar Tad and his pa jest better hide out fer a spell," she heard someone say. Trying to ignore this and direct her aunt back to the parsonage, she missed any further remarks. She noticed that there were several earnest discussions going on.

After their noon meal and after her aunt had retired to her room for a nap, Ann cornered John and asked him if he knew anything about an impending visit by the federal agents.

"I have been expecting an investigation ever since Mr. Price killed those two men," John explained. "Word was bound to get to the officials. I'm surprised that it took this long." He sat down heavily at the kitchen table. He felt Ann should not have to face any more worries right now. Maybe her aunt was right. Maybe he should let her go back to Denver to have their baby.

That afternoon he rode up to Bud's to see what he thought might happen if the federal authorities should come.

"I think someone should ride up and warn them," he told

John. "Price ought to know the danger he's in right now. I'll go tell him, Preacher. Ye need to stay home."

"Bud, do you believe in Price and his still?" John asked the hill man.

"No, Preacher, but ye know Tad's father makes good stuff that won't kill ye, not like some of the rotten stuff I know."

Going inside to Hattie, John asked her to pack a lunch for Bud. "Don't say anything even to Lettie May. We don't want this to get around."

When John returned to the parsonage, he told Ann briefly about Bud going to warn the Prices. With relief Ann told him she was glad he didn't go himself. She believed that the old Granny was up close to the mill too.

It seemed to Ann that the shadows fell more quickly that evening and that there was a real chill in the air. Fall was here and winter would soon arrive. It was good Aunt Cora was leaving. Helping her pack, Ann felt guilty. Aunt Cora had been so generous to her and Ann was all she had. She must have looked sad because her aunt commented.

"Now child," she commanded, "I want you to have John phone if you need me to come back. God knows I hate to go and leave you in this forsaken place. But I can see that there is no use trying to get you to go home with me. Bill told me all about you. He called me you know. I didn't think I should tell him where you were but he found out some way. You see, dear, he is still in love with you. I fear your John is a dreamer. You never will have a decent life living here, but now I guess it is too late because of your baby."

Ann's heart pounded as she listened to her aunt. She had not suspected her aunt had seen or heard from her former lover. Thank God she had not mentioned this in front of John.

"Oh please, Aunt Cora, don't ever mention this to John. He thinks I am so good, and I hope he never finds out about Bill. I do love my husband. He does not know Bill came up here to find me. I told him to never come back and that we were through. I hope he does not hear about the baby." She stopped, afraid she had said too much. If her aunt had noticed she made no comment, and went on with her packing.

"I want you to go in to Siloam Springs and have a good checkup. I should make you go before I leave, but I promised to be back in time for the charity drive next week." Then she added, "I won't be seeing Bill, but if he does call again I will not tell him a thing. I'll just report how happy you are here. You are, aren't you child?" Those penetrating eyes pinned Ann down.

"Of course I am, Aunt Cora. My life has never amounted to much, but now I feel needed. John is a good man and he is gentle and kind to me. I have never been a good person like him. I have always thought of myself first. I still get mad some, but I am trying to change and make John happy here and help him." She felt the tears sting her eyes and averted her face. "Aunt Cora, I do appreciate all you have done for us here. You have been like a mother to me." As they embraced each other, Ann felt a new peace. Surely she could face any trials ahead.

On the following morning John loaded Cora into the spring wagon for the trip to meet the mail truck. As Ann said goodbye, she felt a new affection for this dear woman who had cared for her most of her life. She stood waving as long as Cora's erect figure was visible and the wagon disappeared around the bend in the trail. Soon she was lost in her own reverie.

Catching sight of a bluejay, she told him what a pretty coat he was wearing. She was rewarded by his scolding cries of warning against a hawk that was circling their clearing. Sometimes, she thought, life was too beautiful. Very soon she would have her own child to share this beauty and peace with. If only nothing happened to mar that bright prospect. Then she remembered old Granny Shook. Still what could she do to her now?

Walking slowly, she realized that the swelling of her body was beginning to tell on her strength. She walked back to the porch and began to think about what to have for supper.

As John asked grace over their food that evening, she could see that he was worried over something.

"It seems to me that Bud should have returned by now," he began cautiously.

"Maybe he went on home," Ann suggested.

"No, he wouldn't do that. He knows that I would want to know if he told Price. I wonder how the old man took the news." Then not wanting to worry Ann, he changed the subject.

As the meal ended they decided to sit out on their porch and watch the stars come out. Soon they heard the bullfrogs down on Burnt Creek start their evening concert. To the east, a hoot owl called and was answered by another across the hollow. As the crickets began their serenade, Ann saw the white plume of their friendly skunk edge around the house to find the handout she had left for him.

This was a different world. Not like any she had ever known. It seemed as if she could reach up and touch the stars. It was almost perfect, she reflected. The only bad thing was the superstitions that affected each man, woman, and child. The cure for this, of course, was education. She had been surprised to learn how few adults could write their names, or even read their Bibles. As if reading her thoughts, John spoke.

"The greatest need here is for an adult school," he told her. "If we could teach older folk to read, they would soon learn that spells and charms are wrong." John's big hands were clenched, thinking about how he wanted to do so much here for these people. Surely there was someway he could remedy it. He knew many of them would come if they had a place of their own away from the young children.

"That is what Aunt Cora said," Ann agreed. "Do you think

she would be willing to help us with one of her charity drives? She loves a good cause."

"If we had a place I think we could get the county to furnish us a teacher," John said excitedly. "You know, Bud is humiliated at times because little Bob and Mary can read now and he can't. The answer for us is right here, Ann. We must do something about this."

During the rest of the evening John explored the possibilities of an adult school, where to have it, and who would attend. It was almost exciting enough to make Ann forget her own worries. Then the baby made its presence known and brought her thoughts back to her uncertain future. She hoped all of John's dreams would come true, including a blue-eyed, blonde son.

⊰ Chapter Twenty ⊱

It was almost daylight when John and Ann were awakened by someone pounding on the front door. With a sinking feeling Ann realized something bad must have happened. As John groped his way to the door, she slipped into her robe and lit the lamp. She heard John talking with men out on the porch and felt the cold air rush in the opened door. John turned back into the room.

"Ann," he spoke hurriedly, "these men and Marshal Pruitt have been on the trail all night. They are on their way up to Price's place on Sawtooth. They need someone to show them the way. I have asked them to have some breakfast first. If you'll start the fire, I'll go out and feed their horses."

With a sense of foreboding, Ann realized that these were the federal men they had heard about on Sunday. She started with the wood range first and soon had a fire burning briskly. Setting the coffeepot on the stove, she then stirred up the coals in the fireplace and added wood to them. She heard them on the back porch as John drew a fresh bucket of water for them to wash up. Looking out the back door, she counted three men besides John.

It looked like John would have to go with them. That meant she would be here all alone. She felt the tension grow as her thoughts ran wild. Ann got them settled at the long table and her composure improved. As they attacked the hotcakes and ham, the youngest man prodded John.

"Have you ever been up to Price's mill?" he asked. His eyes were cold and waiting.

"Yes, I was called up there once," John answered cautiously. "The old man was ill and his son rode down to get me." John did not intend to mention the killings unless he was directly asked.

"Then you probably know about his whiskey operation?" another man pressed.

"Yes, I've heard of them," John admitted. "I did not see any signs of it though while I was at his home."

"We hope to catch him in action," the marshal spoke hopefully. "That is why we rode through Gentry at night. This way maybe nobody will have time to warn him."

Ann glanced at John and hoped that he would not say anything. Maybe they could delay these men long enough for Bud to get back down the mountain. John must have been thinking the same thing. He asked for another cup of coffee and offered the men some pie. Then, after prolonging the meal as long as he could, he asked her to fix them a lunch. She could see Marshal Pruitt begin to fidget at the delay. Finally they went out to their horses and she handed the bulging knapsack to John.

"I'm sure I'll meet Bud on the way down," he whispered. "I'll send him here to stay with you, dear, so don't worry. You stay in the cabin and don't go wandering off. I'm sure Mr. Price and Tad have taken cover by now and can't be found without hounds."

"Oh, I'm not worried," Ann lied. "Anyhow, I expect Hattie and Jess to come by today or soon. She's better than anyone, even you." And so it was with a sinking feeling that she watched the four men ride out of sight, weaving in and out of the tall pines. Turning to go back inside, she was suddenly afraid, and sank trembling in one of the cane chairs. Why hadn't she gone home with Aunt Cora?

John knew the trail up the mountain well. They rode a gradual ascent through the sassafras bog, through the scrub, then stately pines appeared over the trail. Here the moss looked cool and pine needles gently muted the sounds of the horses' hooves. As they climbed higher the air became colder. Marshal Pruitt called a halt when they passed the fork near the Childers' place. The horses were tiring and wet with lather.

"There's a spring up ahead a short distance," John told him. "We could give the horses a drink and let them rest too."

Pruitt assented and John led him through the trees to a pool just off the main trail. Here water seeped out of the side of a steep cliff and tumbled down in a small waterfall. Ferns and wild blackberry vines surrounded the pool it made. The horses drank gratefully, then whinnied as they raised their heads. They all heard the sound of a rider on the trail. John turned toward the sound, but the marshal raised a silencing hand.

"We don't want our presence known," he stated as he and the other two men held their horses heads.

With relief, John noted the gait sounded like that of a mule as it moved down the trail. He felt sure it was Bud, but he could not say anything. It would not do for these men to know that Price had already been warned. Bud would soon be with Ann, and realizing this, he breathed easier.

Soon they remounted with the marshal bringing up the rear. The breeze gave way to a wind that stirred the evergreen canopy above them. John reasoned that it must be close to noon and pulled out his watch. He'd give them another hour then suggest that they stop and eat lunch. Surely Tad and his father would be safely away by now. He was roused from his thoughts by the warning call of a bluejay. He hoped there were plenty along the trail on up close to the mill. As they climbed higher the pines became sparser and the sun beamed down on them. Finally Pruitt decided that they could take time for a quick lunch.

As they ate, John took a closer look at his companions. Marshal Pruitt was a sparse man, nondescript in appearance. In fact, he did not look like a lawman. The older man, the one called Clements, looked more in character. He had a keen eye and had not missed much along the trail. He had mentioned that someone had ridden up that way the day before. John decided that the third man, whose name he had missed, was either ignorant or not very talkative. One thing was sure: they were here to find the still. No one had referred to any killings. Feeling Clements' gaze on him, he turned to face him.

"Reverend Nilson, just what do these people live on?" he asked. "I don't see much in the way of crops."

"It's mostly trade and barter in these hills," John explained. "They sell a little tobacco and trade their eggs and butter in Gentry for sugar, flour, and coffee. Quite a lot of fruit is grown and there is some fur trapping. A truck picks up their fruit and pelts and takes them to Siloam Springs. I've been trying to get some of them to put in good apple trees. They only have poor, scrub trees now because they don't know how to use fertilizer. It is cold enough here to produce excellent apples. The blackberries are a good crop too, and they grow good sweet potatoes."

"Do they raise any cattle or hogs for market?" Pruitt asked.

"Mostly just hogs," John answered. "The calves don't get enough of the right feed to bring top prices. Now down close to Siloam there are some cattle."

"Sure looks like slim pickings to me," Clements muttered as he rose and stretched. "Say, Pruitt, ain't it time we got back on the trail?" The marshall nodded, giving the older man a hard look. John saw the dislike between them.

When they remounted, Pruitt and the two men checked their rifles. Clements seemed to be studying the trail and steep ascent.

"How much farther would you say it is?" he asked John.

"Maybe an hour or less," John told him. "It usually takes about five hours."

"Well, we better get with it," Pruitt directed,

They continued single file up the trail and the terrain became rougher. John could see that Clements was getting as edgy as a bulldog on a scent. Looking back into the valley below he wondered how Ann was. He worried too about the Prices. Surely they had taken Bud's warning and left the mill. He hoped they had not hidden in the cave behind their cabin. Marshal Pruitt would surely find the opening. This same trail led up and over the mountain then down to the Missouri line. Many folks on the western side of Sawtooth came up the mountain not only for Price's whiskey, but to grind their grain or to use the lumber saws there.

John was relieved when they finally reached the clearing. Off to the left he heard a sound like sawing. Noting the surprised expressions of his companions, he explained.

"That is not the mill, it is ravens. They are probably feasting on some dead animal. There goes another one to join them. That sound you hear is partly them and also wild turkeys down in that hollow."

"Man, this here must be a hunter's paradise," the third, quiet man remarked.

"We got no time for dreaming," the marshal warned in a low, clipped tone. "There's our cabin." His eyes were as hard as granite as he motioned them on.

"John could not see even a whisper of smoke coming from the crude, rock chimney. Riding in closer he saw that the door was shut and that quilts covered the windows. The only life visible was mountain wrens busily stripping the berries from the holly trees which shaded the south window of the cabin. Dismounting quickly, Clements strode to the door and tried to open it. Feeling it give, he turned back to the marshal.

"Go on in, you fool. We're right behind you," Pruitt barked. John felt his irritation. The birds flew away in alarm and the trees seemed to stop rustling in the quiet of the moment. All their rifles were aimed at the window and door.

"They might be down at the mill," John heard himself saying. His nerves were jumping. Clements walked cautiously around to the back and reported there weren't any other doors.

Pruitt, who knew about the arrangements of moonshiners, told them there had to be a tunnel inside somewhere. One by one they entered the cabin. During the seemingly interminable wait, John was sure they were exploring the tunnel and figured they would find the old man's whiskey cache. Finally they came out the door and the marshal closed it carefully behind him.

"Now, Preacher, show us where the mill is," Pruitt ordered without a word said about what was found inside.

"It is just up this trail on the far side of the clearing," John directed. "You can hear Bitter Creek from here." He saw Clements studying the earth around the cabin, and knew he had seen Bud's tracks. Riding up to the mill he felt divided: part of him was on the side of law, and part of him wanted Tad and his father to get away. I am not a very good man of the faith, he reflected. He either had to be for the right, or he wasn't. There was no standing ground in the middle. He wasn't the same person that had come up here over a year ago. In his mind he saw so many faces: the shiftless one of Will Perkins, the kind face of Hattie Wilks, Bud Childers with his ever-present bulge of tobacco in the corner of his mouth, and old Eli Tate with the gleam of hate in his eyes. These people had worked a change in him. He remembered the shock of finding Sarah Matthews in her bed and the snarl of the yellow cat when he was thrown off the mare.

He could see the grief in Katie's face when they took her baby away to be buried. He remembered the light in Tom's brown eyes when he announced that he was going to become a doctor. There was the answer for him also! He would be the best preacher he could because these people needed him.

As they approached the mill perched beside the rushing mountain stream, John heard the wheel turning fast. The front door was open and the old bench waited invitingly under the shade of the tall pines. Again the marshal and Clements dismounted and walked warily toward the door. John and the other man waited motionless on their horses. A thick covering of sawdust and chaff lay on the ground around the steps and the two staring windows were shrouded by it. John could see many tracks and knew that there had not been any grinding done lately. Glancing upward, he noticed that there were not more than a couple of hours of daylight left. He offered a silent prayer that Tad and his father would not be caught. He knew Pruitt would soon start looking for the still.

"Lets get down and stretch," his companion suggested as he slid off his mount. Gratefully John agreed and dismounted. He was surprised to find that his soreness and stiffness was intensified by his jangled nerves. He would be glad when this trip ended and he hoped he would not have to come up here again for a long, long time.

"Say, these mountains get cold at night," the man shivered.

"That's right," John agreed. "In fact it could be freezing in a month from now. We have rugged winters up here."

"This is my first trip beyond Siloam Springs," the young man volunteered. "I really should not be on this job. Marshal Pruitt lost a man a few weeks ago, so they sent me along to help until he can get a replacement. My name is Rance and I have a family in Little Rock."

"I've been here less than two years myself," John told him.

"In fact, this is my first church. I never in my wildest dreams thought I would land here in these superstitious backwoods."

"I've heard some of the tales about the Ozarks," Rance replied. His voice trailed off as the marshal and Clements came around the side of the mill.

"No sign of Price or his son," the marshal reported disappointedly. "Guess we'll have to start looking for his still. Sure you don't know where it is?" Pruitt looked hard at John.

"No sir, I do not," John answered truthfully and firmly. "His own son, Tad, once told me that he hadn't seen it himself. Mr. Price doesn't trust anyone."

"I'll bet he knows now," Clements said with a short laugh. "Well, let's get started," he told the marshal. "I'll search on this side of the creek and you two go over by this trail. It has to be close to the stream because he would have to have water. I sure don't want to stay on this mountain all night."

"I don't either," Pruitt agreed. "I'll bet a month's pay he's holed up there right now with his rifle primed just waiting for us. I'd like to know who in hell tipped him off." John could not meet his gaze and felt a flush rise in his face.

Marshal Pruitt and Rance walked around the mill while Clements circled the clearing. John didn't know what to do so he decided to sit on the bench and wait. Ann would be worried about him, but he knew she would be safe since Bud would be there. He was worried too about when the baby was due. What if he wouldn't have time to go for Hattie? He had taken a first aid course at seminary, but knew nothing about babies. He wished he had sent her to Denver with her aunt. Suddenly a shout from the marshal interrupted his thoughts.

"Hey, Clements," Pruitt called. "Come have a look at this!" Jumping to his feet, John arrived right behind Clements.

Stepping around them John saw with horror a ball of red hair caught in a blackberry vine on the mill side of the creek.

Feeling faint, he knew with certainty that it was Mrs. Matthews' hair. He clenched his hands inside his coat pockets and tried to compose himself. Clements had registered his expression. The lawman looked straight at him and asked if he knew what the balls were. John hesitated.

"Could be an animal got caught and lost some hair," Rance piped in.

"This is hair, human hair!" Clements snapped. "It's been rolled up like string. Let's see if we can find some more."

John followed Clements down the creek like he was in a trance. Granny Shook was finally getting even with Mr. Price. They would find more that would lead right to the still. John prayed hard that Tad would not be caught and punished for his father's wrongdoing. Soon he heard a shout as another hairball was found.

"Say, somebody sure is on our side," commented Pruitt.

"Could be leading us away from the still, you know," Clements warned.

"I don't think so," Pruitt contradicted. "He must have a few enemies. And one of 'em is helping us. If we don't get going it will get too dark to see," he told them.

The trail was easy as John knew it would be. Twisting in and out of the rustling canopy, it led over an outcropping of rock that would have defied tracking. The men walked so quietly that John felt Mr. Price would never hear them. But they surely knew he was on the lookout. Each man led his horse and spoke softly to them as they slowly looked for the next hairball. They came upon the shack quite suddenly. John saw the brown roof just as Clements gave a soft exclamation. They all stopped. John's mind jumped ahead, wondering if the Prices were inside.

"Now he's not going to take kindly to our visit," Clements warned. "Tie the horses back out of the line of fire, then pick your tree and keep out of sight. I'll work my way around to the rear and cover that."

"Good," agreed the marshal. "I'll give you exactly five minutes, then we will flush them out." Leading his and Clements' horses, Pruitt quietly tied them back out of sight. John waited after hiding the mare.

Those five minutes seemed like an eternity to him. Without his watch he would have believed he had waited an hour. He saw the marshal looking at his watch too. His heart jumped when the call rang out.

"Hello in there, Mr. Price! We know you are in there. I order you to come out in the name of the United States Government." Clements had moved up close in the back. To John the quiet that followed was ominous. If there was anything alive besides the four men, he could not hear or see it. Then he heard Clements repeat the order from directly behind the shack. Nothing moved. Suddenly, the front door seemed to explode as a rifle shattered a limb directly over the marshal's head.

"They're in there," Rance yelled and returned the fire.

"Hold your fire," Pruitt snapped. "Mr. Price, we have an order for your arrest. Come out peacefully and you won't get hurt." The words were hardly spoken before the rifle answered from the shack. John knew that talk was useless, but felt it his duty to try.

"Mr. Price," he called, "this is John Nilson. Please, won't you put your gun away and come on out? You must think of your son, Tad. Surely, you wouldn't want him to get hurt in this trouble."

Dead silence greeted John's efforts, and he could see that Pruitt was getting edgy. Then out of the corner of his eye he saw Granny Shook. She was laughing and jumping up and down back where the horses were tied. Her antics brought her closer with each step.

"Git him! Git him! He be in thar," she screamed. Her evil

face was contorted with hate and her tangled hair danced around her face.

John's skin crawled as he saw her twisted lips and her torn clothing. She must have been sleeping in the forest for days. Then he saw her beckon the marshal to follow as she darted closer still, urging them to shoot.

"He's in thar," she screamed. "I seen him go, and he hain't come out!" As if tantalizing her prey, she danced even closer still beckoning the federal men to follow her. Then, to John, it seemed that the whole forest exploded. The rifle spoke from inside the shack and the door opened wider. Mr. Price had found his mark—the slight body of Granny Shook crumbled to the ground. Fast on the report of the first shot came the old man's second as he swung the barrel toward Rance. With horror, John saw Rance fall. His surprised look turned to one of pain. John felt weak and had to hold on to the tree to keep from falling.

"Stay back," Marshal Pruitt warned John. "The old man has gone crazy!"

Then John heard Clements, who had edged around the corner of the shack, shoot. Mr. Price seemed to waver in the fading light. He tried to turn and face the lawman. John saw his lips moving and knew that he was trying to warn Tad. He staggered only a step then fell half inside the shack. John turned to see about Rance as the Marshal joined him. The younger man lay doubled over. When Pruitt turned him over, John saw that he was dead.

"I knew I shouldn't have brought him," said the marshal bitterly. "It was that damned fancy pants sitting in Little Rock who thought me and Clements couldn't handle one lousy moonshiner." He sounded more mad than sorry as he stood up.

John turned toward the cabin and saw Tad kneeling by his father. Clements was going into the shack. John walked slowly over to the boy, not knowing what he should do. He could not tell Tad his father had done wrong and that he was now paying for it. He was not the one to judge Mr. Price. He put his arm around Tad and felt the sobs shake his thin body.

"Preacher," he cried, "they be fixing to take my pa away. Pa shore never wanted to leave his mountain. He told me jest a'fore you'uns come he never would leave. Now he shore won't have to, will he?"

John looked into Tad's brimming eyes. "No Tad," he promised. "He won't ever have to leave now. But his still will have to be destroyed. You know that what your father did here was illegal."

Tad's thin shoulders straightened. "Preacher, I never would dast to make corn likker. I know my Pa shore never should have. My Ma died on account of hit. I shore hated the nights when I heard Pa drinking with mean-looking men, cussing and hollering. I hope they burn this old shack down to the ground." He slumped down once more across his father and sobbed.

John's emotions engulfed him and he felt like weeping also. So much misery caused by whiskey. Tad was the one who had to suffer and he was innocent of any wrong. As John looked around, he saw Pruitt and Clements wrapping Rance in a slicker. Clements came over and picked up Price's limp hand. Without a word he and the marshal strode behind the shack, and soon John heard the sounds of blows and glass breaking. They were destroying the still. Hearing a shout, he walked over to see what had happened. Pruitt and Clements were looking into a partly concealed opening in the side of the mountain behind the shack.

"Here is the tunnel leading to the back of their still," observed Pruitt. "No wonder this place was never found before. We never would have found it either without the help of those red hairballs."

"That's what they were there for," Clements agreed. "They were meant to lead us right in. Price sure made somebody mad and I'll bet it was that old woman." He walked to a corner of the shack and looked out at the trail. "Where is she?" he asked flatly. The marshal and John joined him. The trail was trampled and as they drew nearer they saw the patches of wet blood. A few feet beyond were some blood-spattered leaves, then nothing. Not one sign that anyone had disturbed the brush on either side. John felt the hair on his neck stiffen. He knew beyond a doubt that Granny had been hit hard. Pruitt must have felt the same way.

"I tell you, Clements," he exclaimed disbelievingly, "there just is no way that old woman could have walked off. She took that rifle shot right in the heart, fell, and didn't move." Pruitt's face was ashen.

"Then neither of you saw her get up and leave?" Clements snapped intently at John.

"I didn't," John replied quickly. "I was so worried about Tad that I forgot all about Granny Shook."

"What did you call her?" Clements asked.

"Everyone calls her Granny. She was a midwife in her younger years. Now people say she is strange and that she works spells. You know the superstitions in these hills." John felt stupid under their searching gaze.

"So she was strange, was she?" Clements mused. "Well I wonder just who helped get her away from here. If she took a bullet as you two say, she's got to be plenty dead. Now dead people just don't get up and walk away." Turning to Marshal Pruitt he added, "Let's finish this job and get the hell out of here."

They loaded the two bodies on the horse that Rance had ridden and John took Tad with him back to the cabin. It was almost too dark to see the trail, but Tad directed them.

"We'll have to stay here tonight," Pruitt decided. "We'll bury Price in the morning." They wrapped Mr. Price's body in a quilt and placed it out of sight in the tunnel. They also took Rance's body down and put it in the cold tunnel for the night. Tad built a fire, heated some beans, and fried some onions with potatoes. Cold cornpone and black coffee rounded out their supper. John was so tired that he heard nothing after he laid down on his pallet after dinner.

The next morning he helped them bury Tad's father next to where his mother had been buried so long ago. John grieved for the young man. He certainly had not had a very happy life up here on this mountaintop.

"Don't they have any cemeteries in this county?" Pruitt asked Tad.

"Yes, there's one down very close to my church," John told him quickly.

"Ma told us she'd jest as soon stay up the mountain," Tad explained. "My Pa, now he didn't hold much with any church. He didn't want nobody coming round and crying over her."

"Well son," the marshal said kindly, "just don't ever try starting up that still again. You run your mill and we won't ever have to come calling on you again. I'm real sorry about your father, but you know his making moonshining was the wrong thing to be doing."

"And Tad," John added, putting his arm around the sad boy, "you're welcome at the parsonage any time. If we can ever help you, ride down or send word. I'd sure like to see you in services once in awhile too."

"Reckon as how I jest might come now," Tad agreed. His face brightened. "Hit's going to be a sight lonesome around here with Pa gone." His shoulders drooped and John saw his eyes fill with tears again.

"What about your brothers, Tad? Won't they be back?"

"If'n they do hit won't be fer long. That Jeb and Burl never did like to mill. All they ever wanted was to be peddling Pa's likker." Tad seemed dejected as he thought about the future. John felt his discouragement and hated to leave him alone on the bunk. He was anxious to get back to Ann and had no choice. Soon he heard Clements call and walked on out to join them.

It was still early when the three men rode off in the bright sun with Rance lying across his horse. John hoped that Ann would not see them ride in, but before they had gotten to the shed and dismounted, she called from the porch.

"Go back in and make lunch, Ann. Make extra coffee," he asked from across the yard. He showed the marshal where the hay was, and they forked down some for their mounts. John hurried into the house to face Ann.

"It's all over," he said. "The still has been destroyed and Mr. Price is dead. Before he was shot, he killed one of the government men. It was the young one. Oh Ann, it was awful." He held his head in his hands. "Poor Tad. I've never felt so sorry for anyone in my life." Ann put her arm around him.

"Dear, you couldn't help what happened. What will Tad do now? Do you think he knows enough to run the mill?"

"Yes, I think so. Anyway he says he will try. We buried his father before we left this morning. Oh, I forgot," he added, "Price killed old Granny Shook. You know, we never would have found that still except that there were little balls of red hair all along the way. They led us right to it. Ann, I believe it was the hair from Mrs. Matthews' head!"

"Katie will be glad Granny Shook is dead. She believes that old woman has a lot of evil power."

"She could be right," John agreed. He reluctantly decided to tell her the rest of what happened. "We couldn't find her body after the shooting was over. She had simply disappeared. We all believe she was dead, because Price shot her right in the heart."

"So, she could have been a witch with with evil power after all," Ann stated, looking at him in fear. "You know that's what Kate and everyone else will say."

"Maybe the story won't get out," John said hopefully. "The

marshal and Clements are not going to speak of this and we sure won't." Seeing the men walking over from the shed, he hurriedly went out and drew a bucket of water so they could wash.

After a quick lunch and a canteen of cold water, John got the spring wagon out and turned it over to the marshal.

"We'll send it back from Siloam and you can pick it up at Gentry," he promised. "This man has been dead too long for us to fool around. We'll get him on the train in Siloam but it will take all day to get him to the undertaker. We thank you for all of your help," he added. "Try and keep your mountain dry, preacher." Both he and Clements smiled at the joke and rode off with the body of Rance covered up in the bed of the wagon.

John saw that Ann looked troubled when they went back inside. She ignored the clutter of dirty dishes on the table and sat down in her high-backed rocker in the front room.

"What is it, dear? Are you feeling bad?" he asked gently. He knew that hearing the news had upset her.

"John, I feel as if I could just sink right into this floor and stay there. I wish Katie and Tom were here. I keep thinking about that old woman and wondering if she is really dead. John," she turned toward him with real fear, "do you believe she was a witch?"

"Now Ann, you know how I feel on that subject," he began. "It is true that people do sometimes seem to have Satan working through them. But the witchcraft around here is mostly superstition in these people's minds. Still, I don't know what happened to her last night." John was truly puzzled.

Ann continued to sit and rock in front of the fireplace, so John decided to clear the table himself. It was not very cold yet and he hurried so he would have time to bring in wood for the evening. He was about to go out for a bucket of water when he heard Ann gasp. He rushed in to her—she was doubled up in the big rocker. Taking hold of her shoulder, he felt her stiffen.

"John," she cried, "you must get Hattie. It's the baby!"

"Are you sure?" he asked in alarm.

"Yes! Look!" She stood up and he saw the pool of water spreading under the rocker. "Hattie said that my water would break first!"

"I can't leave you until Kate comes home," John objected as he grabbed her hands. "Now Ann, you know you can't stay alone. Katie will be back today. She said so."

"I'll be alright. The pains have only started. It usually takes several hours to have a baby. You can be there and back before it will be time."

"But dear, I'm afraid to leave you," John argued. His blue eyes were round with fear. "What if you are one of those women that don't take very long?"

"And what if you have to be my nurse?" she cried. "How would you make out delivering this child? For God's sake get out of here! Every minute could count," she added.

"I'll go, I'll go," John decided. "You go in and lie down. There should be some brandy that Hattie left in the kitchen. Go ahead and drink it." Giving her a small kiss, he built a quick fire and lit it. Ann could not bear to lie down and was soon back in the rocking chair. Giving her final instructions, he ran out and got on the mare, forgetting the saddle. With luck he should make it in an hour to Hattie's.

⚜ Chapter Twenty-One ⚜

It seemed to Ann that the whole world was silent after John banged the kitchen door. How she wished for Katie. What would she do if the baby did come quickly? It looked like she was getting paid back now for her past sins. She deserved any pain she might have to bear. She had always hated a cheat and she was one herself. Lately she had tried to excuse her own behavior but in her mind she knew she was guilty. Granny Shook had gotten to her at last and Ann knew it. Well, she would pay and hope that John did not find out. She got up to walk around, but came back to the rocker again. If only this child could be fair… real fair. Oh God, let John have his little blonde son.

Suddenly pain gripped her again, and her fear intensified. She knew Hattie would not get there in time. She longed for the big, four-poster bed at home in Denver, and the comforting presence of Aunt Cora. The pain ebbed and Ann decided to get a cool drink. John had left in such a hurry the bucket had not been filled. She picked it up, went out on the porch to the well, tied the bucket to the rope, then lowered it. After drawing it halfway up, the pain came again. She lost her grip and the bucket plummeted to the bottom. Gripping the rough stones, Ann realized that the contractions were harder and closer together. She tried to pray but was unable to concentrate.

When relief finally came she retrieved the bucket and poured half back before carrying it to the kitchen. There, she searched for the brandy but failed to find it. Suddenly, she remembered the wild licorice tea that Hattie had left for Kate.

"If'n ye cain't git me, jest keep a mite of spike tea handy," she had advised them. In her frantic search for the little jar, Ann tumbled things to the floor, wincing as one of her good china cups fell and broke. She finally found the little bottle and tugged at the lid. Before she could get it open the awful pain returned. She sank into the cane chair and clung to the table. She tried to count and believed the pain lasted a full minute. When it was over she poured some of the dark liquid into a cup and filled it with hot water. Hurrying into her bedroom she drank the awful tasting stuff. That ought to kill anything, she thought. As the minutes ticked away she lay on the bed, alternately gripping the headrail, then sinking down for blissful minutes into the soft quilts. She lost all track of time and it seemed that a pain hardly ended before another one began. The room rotated in a haze, her heart beat hard, and she knew time was against her.

Ann realized it was slowly becoming dusk. She wanted to light the lamp on the bedside table, but could not will her hands to do it. It was then that she heard someone speak her name. Opening her eyes in hope, her heart seemed to stop. There at the foot of her bed stood Granny Shook. Her evil face leered at Ann through the dusk.

"Heh, heh, ye hain't feeling so pert now, air ye? Now ye can pay fer all yer mean tricks. Ye ain't so goody-goody now. And when thet preacher heers all I tell him, he ain't going to think ye be so good any more." The old woman was dancing around the end of the bed. Ann noticed her clothes were torn and bloody. John had been wrong. She was not dead. As the pain gripped her again, she heard Granny's awful laugh. If she told John about Bill, it would be her finish here. No man would forgive what she had done. Between pains she tried to pray. But would God even listen to her? Old Granny was so right. She deserved just what she was getting.

It seemed forever until she seemed to hear John's voice. From her daze she felt the hot searing of brandy on her lips as Kate held her head up. Then a heavenly, cold cloth wiped her hot face. Now she would be safe, she thought fleetingly. The stark terror was gone, but the gripping pain remained. She remembered Jennie Perkins the night little John was born. Now she knew what Jennie had meant when she said that birthing wasn't ever easy. Reality intruded once again and Ann asked for John.

"He's putting up the mare," Katie replied. "Ye must bear down, Miss Ann," she said.

Ann didn't know how to push or bear down. She clung to the brass bed rail over her head. She felt spent and wasn't sure she had enough strength to even breath. Was she going to die? Maybe the old witch had put a curse on her too. What a fool she had been. She had heard that babies were born easily in nice, clean hospitals, with loving nurses and pleasant doctors. That is where she should be!

"Push, Miss Ann," she heard Hattie coaxing her. "Don't draw in your breath that way. Just breath deep and push."

The last few minutes seemed like one deep well of pain from which there was no escape. Finally relief came and Katie cried, "Thar hit be."

Ann lay back exhausted. Struggling to see, she knew that they were doing something to the baby. Then she heard an electrifying wail as they made it cry. It seemed to be hurting. Well she really didn't care, she felt so tired. If they would all just go away she wanted to sleep for a week. The last thing she heard was Katie laughing.

"Hit be a girl, Miss Ann. Ye got a purty girl baby."

Wincing, Ann felt like she had let John down again. Well, it probably wouldn't matter. By the time Granny Shook got through telling him all about Bill, he wouldn't want her or the baby. It seemed like a short time until she was awakened by a hum of voices. It seemed to come from the kitchen. The lamp had burned low, the bright moon shone through the window and touched the foot of her bed. She felt a need to see someone so she called out. Hattie was first through the door with John and Katie close behind.

Hattie turned up the lamp and smiled at Ann. "Ye got a purty little young'un," she said. "I shore wished we'uns had made hit sooner. But ye made hit jest fine," she beamed.

"John, please John, have you seen her?" Ann spoke low as he came to her side. "John, she was here. Did you see her?" she asked again.

"If'n ye mean thet mean, old womern, we did see her for shore," Hattie said. "And ye don't have to worry no more. The good Lord done took care of her."

"What does she mean, John?" Ann asked.

"Dear, I guess she wasn't dead after all up at Prices'. We found her on the trail not far from here. She was lying right there, all bloody, and still warm. She must have only been dead a few minutes. It was almost like she was waiting for us. Did you say she had been here?" he asked in alarm, taking her trembling hands.

Then the old witch didn't get to tell him anything, she realized. God! She had been saved! Maybe her life here would be worth something after all. Still, there was a burning question in her mind.

"Hattie, how does our baby look? Is it alright? How big is it?"

"Why Miss Ann, hain't ye seen the purty little young'un yet?"

Going over to the crib in the dark corner of the room, Hattie picked up the infant and put it beside Ann. "Why, this is a perfect little baby as ever I've seen."

Ann took a deep breath and pulled the blanket back from the little face. What hair there was amounted to only a golden fuzz. Perfect little hands lay on the blanket. Touching the little nose roused her, and her eyes opened. They were blue! This could not possibly be Bill's child. God had smiled on her at last. It had only been seven and a half months since Bill had been there. This child was so perfect, it could not be an early baby.

"What air ye aiming to call hit?" Katie asked eagerly.

"Yes, dear, our daughter needs a pretty name," John added.

Ann smiled as she studied the tiny face. A beautiful new life, so innocent. Her pardon from God. Could she live up to this enormous opportunity?

"She be born in the full of the moon," Hattie said.

"Now, Hattie," Ann laughed. "I can't believe any bad luck will come from that. John, let's wait and think about a name. You see, I was expecting a son." She smiled at the circle of faces around her.

"There hain't no hurry," the hill woman agreed. "Hit shore cain't make no difference if'n ye wait a day or so."

"Jest so ye do hit a'fore Sunday," Katie interrupted. "Tom be coming then to take me to Siloam. Then we aim ter take a trip on the train soon to Little Rock. Hain't thet going ter be a sight!" Katie's face was filled with wonder.

"Oh Katie, are you leaving that soon?" Ann turned in disappointment to John.

"Now don't ye fret," Hattie said to Ann. "I aim to bring Lettie May to stay fer a spell. Then that Tad Price won't have so fur to ride." She gave them a sly wink.

"That boy is going to be very lonely now," John observed. "I hope he will come down and attend church some."

"Do you think he can run that mill by himself?" Kate asked.

"I think he can," John answered. "I know he looks young, but his father had him doing everything, even running the saws."

"I don't think Tad would ever want to make whiskey even if he could," Ann spoke up.

"If he ever did, it wouldn't be that rotten kind that kills," John said defensively. "It seems to me that somebody will always make it somewhere in these mountains."

"Well, Preacher," Hattie exclaimed, "hit sounds ter me like ye have finally become a mountain man. When ye first preached ye was hellbent agin even smelling a little moonshine."

Amid the general laughter Ann saw that John was trying hard to keep his dignity and decided she should come to his rescue. She knew she really cared how he felt.

"I'll have to give a vote of thanks to Hattie's blackberry brandy. It sure was a help," Ann told them.

"Hit ain't no sin ter take spirits," Hattie stated. "Why thar be sin and evil in a feller eating like a hog, or running off at the mouth agin folks."

"I'm inclined to agree with you," John said thoughtfully. "Not that I will ever condone moonshining." He looked at them all seriously when they laughed again.

It was close to noon when Hattie drove away in her wagon promising to bring Lettie May back on Sunday. Tom was due before then and he and Kate would be leaving the hollow early the next Monday. Propped up like a queen, Ann surveyed her devoted subjects. John was running in and out, partly to ask if he could be of service, but mostly to get a look at the sleeping baby. Ann felt at peace with the world. Yet something still was gnawing at her insides. What was she worried about? She didn't have to be afraid of the old hag anymore and her baby could not be Bill's. She had already decided that she loved this preacher, and wanted to make him happy. So why was she so nervous anyway? There were still lots of problems here, she knew. And of course John felt responsible for all of these people. He would be worrying about Tad and Lucy Tate. He had already stuck his nose into the Holcomb and Jones feud. She knew in her heart that she had not been honest with John. He deserved so much better than her. Damn, she guessed the time had come. She couldn't live with the lie between them.

It was when the birds started singing outside her window that the name for their child came to her. Robin! Robin! Little blue-eyed, golden-haired Robin. She called to John and asked him if he liked it. Seeing the delight in his eyes, she became serious. This would be the hardest thing she had ever had to do in her life. What if he was so hurt he would not want to continue their life here together. At least she had a hold on him through little Robin.

"John," she began nervously, "I have to tell you something. I am so ashamed of what I have done. I should have told you about it long ago. I hope you won't hate me, but I can't live with this guilt any longer. I just hope..."

"Ann," John interrupted. "Whatever you have to tell me doesn't matter. I love you more now than I did when we first met. Surely there is nothing you can say that will make any difference." He knew in his mind what was coming.

"John, please let me finish," she sobbed. "If I don't tell you now, I'll never find the courage again." Clasping her hands hard, she looked up at this blonde giant standing over her. "You see, before I ever met you I had a lover. He said he loved me and wanted to take care of me. I had never had anyone to care for me other than Aunt Cora. I was just starved for love. I found out too late that Bill didn't want to get married. He just wanted a playmate. We did have fun. He was wealthy and took me everywhere. Some of my friends were scandalized and so was my aunt. I thought it was enough until I met you. John, I didn't know what love was until you. Oh John, can you ever forgive me?" She buried her face in her hands.

John stood trembling by the bed, not knowing just how to begin. He had dreaded this moment, knowing that if she really loved him, that some day she would confess. He had prayed that she would get over this man, Bill. His prayers had been answered at last. Surely she would never leave him now. Sitting down beside her he gently raised her face and looked into her tearful eyes.

"I knew all about Bill a long time ago," he stated quietly. "And I have prayed every day since I met you that you would forget this man and love me alone."

"You knew? Who told you? Aunt Cora promised me she wouldn't say a word. How could you love me if you knew what a bad person I was? You are a preacher!"

"It doesn't matter, dear, who told me. I didn't believe the story at first. I thought it was just someone who was jealous of you repeating gossip. But I checked around and found out it was really so. Ann, I loved you from the minute I first saw you walk across the dance floor. I prayed about you. Somehow I knew you were meant to be my life partner. I know it has been hard for you here with no conveniences at all, and such hard winters. But I will do better some day. I don't know how much longer I will be here in the Ozarks. There is so much I want to do here for these people. And I need your help, Ann."

"I will help, John. I will." She knew a new determination at that moment. So some of her dear, sweet girlfriends had tried to ruin her chances with John. She had known they envied her luxuries while living with Bill, but never dreamed they could be so vicious. Feeling so relieved to get her guilt off her mind, she saw that John was trying to say more.

"Ann, I have to tell you something else," He stood irresolute, hating to bring out the secret that had been worrying him. "You see, the church in Denver that wanted me to come over a year ago, still wants me." Seeing her guilty face he hastened on. "Your aunt let it slip when she was here. I was so happy that you had chosen to stay here then. But now with our little baby, I want you to think it over carefully. I'll understand if you decide to leave."

Oh God, she thought. So here it was again, up to her. She would love to go back to civilization. Then looking up at John's strained face, she knew she could not hurt him again.

"Dear, I want what you want. I know how you feel about these people. We'll stay until you feel you can leave in peace. Until the adult school is built and classes are started, until you get some orchards started, and until Tom can come back and take part of your work over, we'll work together." She saw the glow on John's face. Still, she wondered if he knew of Bill's visit. Well, she would not ask. Looking out into the blue haze across the hollow, she felt the magic of the hills. Here she would learn at last how to become an honest, caring wife and mother.